MINDY HAYES

GLIMMER

A Faylinn Novel

Published by Mindy Hayes
Cover design and photography by Regina Wamba of
www.maeidesign.com
Edited by Madison Seidler, Madison Says

ISBN: 1540363708
ISBN-13: 978-1540363701

To my readers

ONE

SARAI

Snow gently drifted onto the mountaintops of Rymidon as I watched from the window of my tower nestled within the crevices of the mountainside. Waterfalls frozen mid-stream down the rock, reminded of my life—immobilized, stagnant. I had hope in a better tomorrow, but since returning from Faylinn I'd found myself spiraling into depression. Thankfully, the winter would not last much longer. I missed the green. The cold matched my stage of mourning. I needed the warmth to thaw my sadness, to remind me of what I had to live for.

Focusing on each snowflake falling to the earth was calming. It'd been a month since The Battle of Faylinn. Since I'd lost the rest of my family, since I'd become one fae responsible for so many. While I mostly mourned the loss of Sakari, I couldn't help but grieve for my father and Skye. Not only for their lives lost, but also for the lives they'd taken. For the men they chose to be as opposed to the men they could've been. I mourned for all that could've been.

It has been a trial to stay strong for Rymidon as they have needed me most while we try to rebuild the kingdom we once knew. When I stood at my window and saw them working as one, it made it easier for me to push forward and see the importance of my role. They were the hope. I was the guiding light. Though, most days it felt like I was nothing more than a flickering candle.

"Your Grace." I peered over my shoulder to see Kayne in the tall stone archway. He bowed lowly.

"Yes, Kayne," I said kindly, though tired.

He stood at attention and took a heavy breath. "There has been an incident."

I turned all the way around to face him. "What sort of incident?"

"Brae and Gallagher stumbled upon one of our own on their patrol of the forest this morning."

I waited for him to continue, giving him a look to show I was ready for whatever he would deliver. I could take it no matter how bad. *How much worse could it get?*

"His throat was slit." Kayne paused. "He was drained of all his blood."

Could we not live in peace for more than a month? Must we already turn on one another?

"Who was it?"

"Eldon of the Sowers."

"Zanna's betrothed," I presumed. My heart ached for her. He nodded, firm.

"Who knows about this?"

"Brae and Gallagher came straight to me. I told them to

keep it quiet until we knew more."

"Good. Keep it that way. I don't want there to be needless upset in the kingdom until we get down to the bottom of it."

"Yes, Your Grace."

"Are there any indications of who might be responsible?"

"There was no weapon on the grounds, nor any disturbance of the land. It was as though he was killed elsewhere and left in our forest."

"Can you tell me anything else? Do you believe it was the work of one of our own?"

His head shook once, confidently. "No. I do not see why anyone would after we lost so many in the battle. It was not as though it was done out of passion. With his body completely drained, it was almost as if he were killed for his blood. I do not see why any of the other kingdoms would take such an action, unless it was a rogue faery."

Letting out a breath, I asked, "So, what do you gather, Kayne?"

"I cannot say for sure, Your Grace, but I believe it was an outsider. Who? I do not know yet, but I have every Keeper looking out. We will get to the bottom of it. I promise you."

Kayne had kind eyes—always had. When I was locked away for my supposed protection, it always made me feel calmer knowing he was on post. Even as he stood before me, declaring his promise of justice, there was no malice or hate in his eyes, only concern and determination.

"Thank you, Kayne. You may go."

He offered a close-lipped smile and bowed as he backed out of the room, shutting the door behind him

No matter where my head or heart was, my time to step out

of my stupor was now. I could no longer dwell on the past. I needed to be present for my kingdom. It was time I truly accepted my place as Queen of Rymidon.

TWO

CAMERON

"Lia, if you're going to live in this world, you'll need to get your butt off my couch and find a job. You can't keep living with me and expect me to do everything for you."

Though Calliope had never actually asked me to, it had been implied. *Look out for her, Cam.* Not that I understood why, after all Lia had put her through, but when Lia had shown up on my doorstep a couple days after I'd arrived at Clemson, with a sigh I'd opened the door wide and let her pass by me. *What else could I do?* I hadn't even questioned how she'd found my apartment. *Who knows what she's capable of?* Pretty much anything.

"I'd be happy to find a job. If you can find a place that will hire me, I'll take it," she mumbled as she scrolled through the channels, not once looking at me standing by the armrest. Her legs stretched out on the ottoman, crossed at the ankles.

This was her assumed position every day. *Can I really be surprised to find her this way again?*

"Do you have a resume?" I asked.

She snorted. "And what would you suggest I put on it? 'Evil former faery with a horrible track record of lying and deceit, seeking a position at your fine institute.'"

"Well, that's a start," I said. "Though I'd leave off the whole horrible track record part. That won't get you in the door anywhere, but since you've got the whole lying and faking part down, you'd be perfect in sales or customer service, blowing smoke up people's butts all day long. Tell them you've never had a job before, but you're very motivated."

Lia lifted a dry look. "I'm working on it, Cameron."

"I can see that. Is it telepathic job hunting? If it is, I'm impressed. I hadn't realized faeries had that ability."

"I don't understand how you still remember everything," Lia muttered, averting her gaze. "It's been months. You're a human. I'm a human. You're supposed to forget these things. Why can't we be human beings like everyone else?"

"I think it's kind of hard to forget when my best friend is the faery queen you tried to screw over."

Lia rolled her eyes and settled further into the cushions, crossing her arms over her chest. Her eyes saddened, and I felt a little guilty for throwing that at her. Not that I've forgiven her, but a part of me feels bad for her. Even though she did it to herself, Lia has no one. And if Calliope was able to forgive, I need to try, too.

I decided to answer her honestly. "I'm thinking it's like Calliope's mom being aware of the existence of faeries through all those years because Finn still had a hint of faery blood in him. And they hardly spent any time apart. Since you're around me all the time—I assume there's still some faery blood running through your veins—I haven't been given the opportunity to forget."

"I thought Finnian was special because of his Royal bloodline," she argued. Everything was an argument with her. We could never have a civil conversation. Every word out of her mouth was laced with superiority or irritation. Granted everything out of my mouth was sarcastic, but that was beside the point. She provoked me. I couldn't help it if my tongue had a mind of its own.

"What do I know, Lia? I'm a mere mortal on planet Earth. I just live here." When she didn't respond, I said, "Look, I need to get to class. You going to be okay?"

A look that was less than amused enflamed her eyes. She blinked once, but said nothing.

I cleared my throat. "I'll take that as a yes."

"I'll survive." She focused on the TV once again. "If I don't, I doubt that would cause any issues for you."

True. "Well, at least we agree on something. I'll see you later." I saluted her and walked out the front door.

THREE

LIA

The apartment door shut. Finally, alone again. It was rare to be by myself in his apartment. With Cameron's two roommates always coming and going, I rarely had a moment alone.

Nothing on TV was even remotely interesting—not that is ever was. Just a bunch of people playing a part for others' entertainment. Look where pretending to be someone else got me. I grabbed my jacket and decided to head out. We weren't far from the forest, and that was still the only place where I felt comfort. Where I felt home.

There were times when I'd sit cross-legged at the edge of the trees and do nothing but stare. Some might have found it boring or strange. I found it soothing. And complete torture. Though, it was worse to stay away.

I missed the feel of the wind blowing through my hair

and across my wings as I soared through the branches and vines. I missed the soft touch of moss beneath my feet, the taste of vigas and pruillas on my tongue. I missed … Skye. I was fully aware that I shouldn't. But even after all he'd done, I still loved him. And I lost him, too.

What I wouldn't give to have my wings back, to have their encircling comfort around my body. I needed their comfort now more than ever. I was alone. Alone in a gigantic world I didn't know how to belong to anymore.

Sure, I'd lived here for a time before, but I had been acting. I'd had a make-believe family and friends. I'd had school, somewhere to go, a schedule. I'd had a place to call home. This time, I felt lost. As much as I didn't want to admit it, I needed Cameron. I couldn't survive on my own.

For the first couple weeks, I'd sought shelter in the forest across from Cameron's house. I wasn't sure how I'd ever thought sleeping in a tree was comfortable before. After the first night, my back was killing me and I was covered in bug bites. When his Dad had left for work and Cameron had left for who knows where, I'd snuck into his house to shower and swipe some food. I'd had no money. No transportation. No clothes aside from the ones I'd been wearing. No form of identification. Eventually, I'd had to stay in a homeless shelter just so I would have a bed instead of a branch to sleep on.

When I'd seen Cameron packing up and leaving for college, I'd known I had to follow. Somehow I was going to suck up my pride and ask for help. I'd had no other choice. There was no way I could survive on my own in the human world. It ran so differently from Rymidon. I couldn't barter my way through life or use my status as the betrothed of a Royal. I was nothing here. A nobody.

Little did Cameron know that I had been trying to get a job, but everywhere I went either wasn't hiring or wanted someone with a degree or at least *some* sort of experience. Experience in anything. I'd tried restaurants, retail stores, offices that might need a receptionist. None of them could understand how a twenty-year-old was searching for her first job ever, not to mention I didn't even have a high school diploma. I mean … I assumed I was twenty in human years. Close to it anyway. I'd only pretended to be younger for my human life before so I could go to high school and be close to Calliope. I suppose I could try to pass for someone younger now. *Would that work in my favor?*

Thankfully, Cameron knew someone who knew someone who had been able to hook me up—for small fee, which Cameron had paid—with a fake ID, birth certificate, and a diploma … to prove I existed.

"Once you get a job, you're paying me back," he'd said.

"Like I want to be indebted to you," I'd retorted.

Granted, I could suck it up and be a bagger at a grocery store or work at a fast food chain, but that kind of money would hardly pay the bills if I wanted my own place, which I needed as soon as possible. I needed something steady if I was going to survive on my own—and that needed to happen soon. I couldn't stand Cameron's judgmental stares every time he saw me, for much longer.

Trust me, Cameron, if I had anywhere else to go that's where I'd be.

My eyes traveled over the vines creeping up the trunks and intertwining with the branches. I missed my life before. I knew exactly what I was giving up. And though I knew, the trees were a part of me. This was my penance. To be within reach of the woodlands and not be able to appreciate them the way I used to.

The leaves crunched, and my eyes shifted. It might not have given anyone else a second thought, but I knew better. I knew what lived in the trees.

Getting to my feet, I let my eyes drift over the branches and shrubs. It was probably smarter to leave, but I was too curious not to stick around. My body took a defensive stance just in case, but then I saw big green eyes and long blonde curls emerge through the vines.

"Calliope?"

"Hey, Lia."

FOUR

SARAI

Kayne followed me down the foliage-covered hillside dusted in snow as we made our way into the village, the rest of my personal Keepers in tow. It was important to me to mingle with everyone daily. I wanted Rymidon to know I was apart of them. While I lived in the castle on the mountainside, high above the kingdom, I was merely a mouthpiece. My role was to create a peaceful, functioning society. This was not a dictatorship. I was here for them. I was not my father, and they needed to know I cared.

Today, I had a secret agenda, but I didn't want to raise any alarm. I needed to know if anyone else was aware of the death, if someone noticed anything out of the ordinary, but I had to be discreet. The last thing Rymidonians needed was to feel hunted in our home.

Before I was able to begin conversations with anyone I

noticed uneasy stares. Did they already know? Was the death revealed without my approval? When I realized they weren't looking at my Keepers or me, I followed the line of sight to a group of fae with vines wrapped up their right arms entering Rymidon. Faylinnian Keepers. A familiar face approached front and center.

"Declan." I smiled. "How nice to see you."

He bowed. "Queen Sarai, Calliope asked that I personally extend an invitation to a celebration in Faylinn. A uniting celebration to bring the kingdoms back together and rebuild amity."

"Is she sure that is wise this soon after The Battle?" Calliope mentioned she wanted to do something like this, but I had not realized she meant to do it so soon. The other kingdoms may need more time to heal before associating with us.

"She knew you might be apprehensive, so she wanted me to assure you Rymidon is welcome. All kingdoms will be aware of your attendance. The hope is they will join with open hearts and minds. She has assured them all of your stance and the peace you seek, as well as the Supremacy Adair abused. They will know Rymidon is no longer a threat."

I nodded and smiled kindly. "Thank you, Declan. I will speak with my kingdom. I do not want to accept an invitation before I know they are comfortable. I'm sure Calliope will understand that. Please extend her my love and gratitude for her efforts."

As the Faylinnians left, Kayne took a step closer to me and bent to speak in my ear. "With the recent assassination, I'm not sure it is a wise decision to accept. There is no way for us to know if it is safe."

"I agree, Kayne," I said quietly and continued walking, smiling and acknowledging fae as we passed their dwellings. "But, the celebration may also be the perfect opportunity to further investigate. What if we are not the only kingdom who lost someone? I will leave the choice up to each member of our kingdom. I will be in attendance. If they chose to stay behind, I will not fault them. I will also ask that we have a solid unit of Keepers that remain behind in case there are any more incidents. I pray this was an isolated incident, but I will not take any chances."

FIVE

CAMERON

"Hey, can I catch a ride home? I rode to class with Ryland."

"Yeah," I said. "Sure."

Chase hopped into the passenger side of my jeep and latched his seatbelt. "So, what's the story with Ginger?"

"Who?" I turned the ignition.

"You know … the red head who's been sleeping on our couch."

"Oh." I sighed. "Lia just needs a place to crash until she gets back on her feet. I told you that."

"Yeah. I know, but she's been living with us for months now. What's her story? Why doesn't she have a place to stay?"

Lia and I had talked about this, the cover story we would tell everyone. Because how was I supposed to explain to everyone that she'd transformed into a human from a faery in order to trade places with my best friend's husband so they could be together? *Husband.* That was still weird to think about. Even though Calliope and Kai had been married for months, it was probably only a couple weeks in Faylinn time. I still didn't know how that worked. Their time was all kinds of skewed.

At first, I could say she'd needed a place to crash for a few nights, but we're *way* beyond a few nights. "She's a drifter. Lia doesn't really have a place she calls home. She likes to move around, not be tied down for long. It's just taken her a little bit longer than usual to decide where she wants to go."

"So, she's like a hippie. That's hot."

That really irritated me for some reason. She wasn't hot. She was a witch. She'd destroyed so many lives. She'd almost gotten my best friend killed. Not to mention, me. I couldn't forget being kidnapped and left to die in Faylinn. All her spying had nearly cost me everything.

"How much longer will she be sticking around?"

Too long. "I dunno. Hopefully, she'll get a job and be gone soon. I'm sorry if she's cramping your style or something."

"Nah. It's cool." Chase shifted in his seat like he was uncomfortable, and then he asked, "You guys have something going on or…?"

"Me and *Lia*? No. No, no, no. No. It's not like that. She used to be friends with my best friend, Callie. But, uh, they've got some awkward blood now and…" *Why was I telling him all of this?* "Anyway, we're just friends. Acquaintances, really."

"So, would you be cool if I asked her out?"

I snorted. *As long as I get a front row seat to her rejecting you.* "Yeah. Good luck." *You'll need it.*

When I walked into my apartment, I found Lia exactly where I'd expected her to be, sprawled out on the couch with her feet propped up on the ottoman. What I hadn't expected to see was Calliope beaming right beside her.

"Cameron!"

"Callie!" I flew across the room as she stood, and took her in my arms. She hugged back—a little too tightly. "Cal," I grunted.

"Oh, right. Sorry," she whispered and loosened her grip. "I forget. You know I'm still not used to my strength."

Callie must have rummaged through Lia's clothes because she was dressed in jeans and a white T-shirt, exactly the way I remembered her before all of this. Her hair was braided on both sides over her ears. It was déjà vu. High school all over again. Her eyes were a little bit bigger and a little bit brighter. Suddenly, I remembered Chase, who was probably observing from the entryway. I turned to see him looking at Calliope with a funny expression. She might've looked a little different, but not enough for him to question *what* she was. At least I hoped not.

She stepped forward with her hand outstretched. "Hi. I'm Calliope."

He placed his hand in hers and shook. "Chase." There was a moment where she looked questioningly at their hands before she smiled reminiscently and let go.

"So, you're Cameron's roommate?" she asked.

"Yeah…" he said slowly, never taking his eyes off her.

He could've been checking her out, or he could've been studying her. Either way, I didn't want him to scrutinize her any longer. This was a huge risk for Callie to take. I wasn't sure why she'd thought it was a good idea to come here. Not that I was complaining. It was always good to see her, but it would probably be a better idea to talk in private. Away from Chase's curiosity.

"Cal, let's go to my room." That sounded inappropriate. I didn't want Chase getting the wrong idea. "Lia, you too." *Not much better, Cameron.* "Let's all go chat."

Callie nodded at Chase. "It was nice meeting you, Chase." I waited to walk down the hallway until I knew she was right behind me. When the three of us were inside, I closed my bedroom door.

"He's going to be questioning his sanity for a few hours." Callie laughed.

"Who are you, and what have you done with my best friend?"

"What?" She continued to chuckle.

"You're not worried about someone questioning your appearance?" I asked, hushed. "All of the people you passed by on your way here? Everyone in this complex? Nothing?"

She shrugged. "It's not like he knew what I looked like before. I can hold my own now, and I'm not staying long enough to give anyone the chance to truly question it."

I sighed, not liking her thought process, but let it slide. "Well, all right. How did you know where to find us?" I tossed my backpack into the corner of my room and settled into the chair at my computer desk.

"Well, when I went to see my mom, she said you'd gone off to Clemson, which I assumed. I asked your dad for your address. I actually didn't know how to find Lia, but I hoped you would know. Oddly enough, I stumbled upon her when I came through the trees."

I cut my gaze to Lia, sitting at the end of my bed. "I see

how it is. Instead of trying to find a job, you've been traipsing through the forest like a wannabe faery. Productive."

"Don't mess with me, Cameron Bennett. So help me, you will regret it."

I chuckled dryly. "I'd love to see what you mean by that. Please. Do share."

"Okay," Calliope interrupted. She put a hand on my chest and outstretched her other to ward off Lia. "So, I came to make sure you two hadn't killed each other yet. Looks like I didn't come a moment too soon."

Lia crossed her arms over her chest and pursed her lips. I rolled my eyes and shook my head. Cal should be more worried about Lia murdering me than me murdering Lia.

"Y'all need a break from the real world? We've got a celebration going on tonight in Faylinn if you want to come."

It was good to hear a hint of her Southern accent again. "Will Sarai be there?" I asked.

"If she is, you won't be getting within twenty feet of her."

"Aw, c'mon, Callie. I won't bite," I teased.

"That's not what I'm worried about, and you know it."

"I promise to be good." I marked an X over my heart and gave my best puppy dog eyes. She couldn't resist those.

Callie narrowed her eyes and wagged her finger. "Don't you dare make that girl fall in love with you, Cam. You'll have to answer to me. I've learned a few things as queen, since we last saw each other. I promise you don't want to answer to me."

"I can't make that promise," I joked, but retracted when Callie sliced me with her stare. "I promise." I nodded like a good boy. "I need to be back by Sunday. You think that'll happen?"

"What day is it?"

"Friday."

She cocked her head and thought for a moment. "Shouldn't be an issue. I'll escort you back right after the festivities end. If worse comes to worst, it'll be Sunday night or maybe early Monday morning. I guess we'll find out."

"I can make that work."

Lia hadn't said a word. "Are you in Lia?" Calliope asked.

She glanced up at Callie, suspicious. "Are you sure that's such a good idea?"

"What do you mean?"

"There's not some bounty on my head? You're not trying to lure me back to Faylinn to get rid of me?"

"What? No! Of course not." The shock that flashed across Callie's face couldn't be mistaken for anything but hurt. "You think after what you did for Kai that I would dream of hurting you? Maybe you could turn your back on someone you care about without batting an eyelash, but I couldn't."

I should be surprised that Callie was so forgiving after what Lia did to her, but I wasn't. Even when we were growing up and got into fights, when it was me who was at fault, she'd be the first to apologize. She might be stubborn, but she was not a grudge holder.

"You'll be under my protection," she assured Lia. "No one would even think about hurting you."

"What's the occasion?" I asked.

"Well, with everyone attempting to get back to normal after the battle, I thought it would be nice to have all the kingdoms together to celebrate uniting as one."

"So, Rymidon will be there?" Lia asked. "You sure that's such a good idea?"

Callie nodded. "Sarai has assured me things are different there. She wants to put the past behind us and move forward."

Lia hesitated. "And I'll have your protection from Rymidon as well?"

Callie's brow furrowed.

"If you recall, I fought on your side in that war. I killed many of my own. They won't take kindly to a traitor."

"Sarai wouldn't allow anything to happen to you. If it makes you feel any better I will have a detail on you all night to ensure your safety."

Skeptically, Lia chewed on her lips, then nodded.

Callie clapped her hands together. "Great! Let's go!"

SIX

LIA

While this wasn't my first time as a human entering the fae world, being on Faylinn soil as a human never lost its luster. Though, I saw and felt everything through different eyes, it was still as beautiful as I remembered. Being away hadn't diminished my memories. In fact, reentering heightened everything—every emotion, every memory, every sense. I wasn't faery, but it felt like the fae blood lay dormant in my veins, begging for release.

As I watched Cameron and Calliope walk side-by-side toward Faylinn, I thought about turning back. They could go on without me. It was unbearable to feel all of this. As wrong as it might have been, my heart ached for Skye more fiercely with every step. And with that, I also felt what could only be described as phantom wings. The way an amputee might feel a leg or arm that was no longer, I felt wings that yearned to soar.

"Lia?" Calliope glanced over her shoulder at me. "What is it?"

Had I stopped? My body knew better. It wanted to turn back. I should've listened. They should go on without me. I'd go back to Cameron's apartment and bask in my loneliness. *Could I be anymore of a coward?* "I don't think I can do this."

"I promised you'd be safe." Calliope stepped closer. "I won't break that promise."

My eyes rested beyond her, watching the sun setting through the trees, illuminating an orange glow between the branches. "It's not that."

Her head tilted to the side, questioning.

I cleared my throat. Did I want to be honest with her? It was habit as her former best friend, to pour out my heart, but as an infiltrator who used to keep so many secrets from her, I wanted to keep my thoughts locked away.

"Being here … it's more difficult than I thought it would be."

I wasn't sure what my face revealed, but Calliope's eyes slanted in understanding. "I can take you back. I only thought you'd want to come, but if it's too much, I'll take you back through right now."

My body split in two, equally wanting to retreat and

move forward. Maybe this was exactly what I needed—one last visit for closure on my past life.

Exhaling, I kept walking. "No, it's fine. Let's go."

Once we reached the outskirts of Faylinn, the peak of the vast valley coming into view, Kai greeted us. He was leaning against a wide trunk, his arms and ankles crossed, bow and arrows slung across his chest.

"Took you long enough."

"Oh, stop." Calliope sighed. "To you, I couldn't have been gone for more than two minutes."

Kai pushed his back off the tree and grabbed her waist, planting a kiss on her mouth. "Two minutes too long." His quiet words were muffled against her lips, but even my human ears could hear him.

Groaning, I couldn't help muttering, "Gag me."

Kai drew back and offered a nod. "Always a pleasure, Lia."

"Wish I could say the same, Kai."

His patronizing smirk never left his face. "Still as delightful as ever. Good to know some things haven't changed. Hi, Cameron."

Cameron gave Kai a nod. Such a guy.

Maybe this was a bad idea. There was no one I wanted to see. If all I had to look forward to were snide remarks and judgmental stares, there was no reason for me to stay. And the pain only became more excruciating the longer I remained in Faylinn. *Why did I agree to come?*

"If it makes you feel any better," Cameron leaned

into me, "I'm not any more comfortable than you are."

"Ha." I didn't want to smile at him, but one slipped past my lips before I could rein it in. I nipped it before it could last long.

The evening began as I'd suspected. Most Faylinnians were not pleased to see me in attendance. As we walked into the meadow I was met with a trail of backs turned and sneers. Some words stuck out more than others.

"Traitor."

"Impostor."

"Liar."

With every glower and hushed whisper, I couldn't help but wonder when someone was going to stab me in the back or shoot an arrow through my heart. But I wasn't allowed to feel wounded. How could I? This wasn't the human world, and I hadn't merely done something petty like spread a rumor or talk behind my best friend's back. I hadn't cheated on my boyfriend or stolen a boy from another. I'd been the fuel behind a war that had killed nearly half of their kingdom. I deserved every hurtful remark.

They were all true.

Before I could prepare myself for the inevitable tension, I watched Sarai approach us with her Keepers in tow. Making myself as invisible as possible, I crept behind Cameron.

"I'm not a human shield," he muttered over his

shoulder.

"Today you are."

SEVEN

SARAI

"Sarai." Calliope smiled. I pulled her in for a tight embrace. Hers was the brightest face I had seen in quite some time.

"Thank you, Calliope. A night away is exactly what our kingdom needs. It is exactly what *I* need."

"I think a night of levity is what all our kingdoms need." She squeezed me before letting go. "I've missed you. Even though you said you'd be here, I was worried Rymidon wouldn't come."

I nodded my understanding. "I will be honest with you. There was some apprehension. A lot of them stayed behind, but I assured them that all you want is peace, as we all do. None of them wanted to hurt anyone while under Adair's Supremacy."

"I know." Calliope offered a sympathetic smile as she

rubbed her hand against my arm. "And my kingdom knows that, as well. I promise you, tonight will be the beginning of putting the past behind us and uniting the seven kingdoms once again."

A throat cleared, and my eyes turned to Cameron standing a few feet from Calliope. How had I missed him? It was difficult to decide what would be appropriate. I wanted to hug him, but a root was most likely best. "Hello, Cameron."

He bowed his head, but not in a way that was normally done. His head knocked back, his chin lifting as he tossed a wave up in the air. My cheeks grew warm. He met my outreached hand, wrapping his fingers around my wrist in a root, leading me to believe Calliope must have taught him the proper way to greet the fae.

"Sarai, it's really good to see you." The tips of his fingers brushed back and forth against the inside of my wrist, tingling my skin. "You're as beautiful as ever."

The smile on my face widened, though I attempted to remain as composed as a Royal should. He was still as charming as before. "And you. It is good to see you, that is. Though, you look great, too." *Oh, dear, Sarai. Keep your mouth closed.*

Cameron jumped, releasing my wrist. "Ouch!" His eyes darted to Calliope beside him.

Calliope smiled at me. "Dang erona bugs. Just as bad as mosquitos. They must love humans, I guess."

"Yeah." Cameron scowled at her. "They feel a lot more like a pinch than a bite."

"And Marcus of Oraelia makes his usual silent appearance," Kai commented, his eyes fixated across the meadow.

I looked over in search of who Kai was speaking about. If it were not for my father keeping me separated from civilization, I might know more about the Royals from the other kingdoms.

A tall, statuesque man with cropped black hair and talon-like earrings pierced through his earlobes hovered on the edge of the gathering. His dark skin was a striking contrast against his forest green eyes and ornate crown of bone.

"Prince Marcus saved my life in the battle." Calliope's voice was small—grateful, yet subdued. Did she think about Sakari, as I did, every time the war was mentioned?

"He did?" Kai seemed surprised. Was that something Prince Marcus wasn't known to do?

Calliope nodded, thoughtful. "I didn't see my attacker behind me. Prince Marcus took care of her with one arrow. He also led one of the companies to bring back the dead and wounded. We've never spoken. I've never been able to get much information about him, but what little I know has impressed me."

Kai slipped his hand around Calliope's, a minor gesture, one he most likely did without thought. An image flashed before my eyes: Sakari standing beside Calliope, holding her hand as he peered lovingly at her. While they were not meant to be, I couldn't help but think of what life could've been like had Sakari lived.

Kai buried his face into her light curls and spoke softly. "I'll have to thank him for being one of many to keep you alive out there." With a soft kiss to her temple, he pulled back.

"He lost someone dear to him in the battle," Lia quietly said. I'd hardly noticed her until now. She was doing an exceptional job of taking cover behind Cameron.

"Prince Marcus?" I asked, giving her my attention. We'd all lost someone to dear to us, but for some reason I wanted to know more about Marcus of Oraelia, about who he'd lost.

Her eyes shifted uneasily between Marcus and me. She refused to meet my gaze, her eyes touching just below mine, and I couldn't fault her. She must have believed I despised her. On the contrary, I hurt for her. We had been close once upon a time. I knew about her relationship with Skye long before my father had exploited it. I could only imagine the amount of guilt she carried around. Why had she not confided in me? I could have been there for her, helped her make the right decision.

Lia cleared her throat and said a little louder, "His best friend, Nerida."

"How do you know that?" Calliope asked.

Lia exhaled and slowly drew her eyes to Prince Marcus. His expression was somber, his eyes slanted at the corners as he surveyed the mass of fae. Or maybe he was angry. The straight line of his lips made it difficult to decipher.

"I watched it happen," she said, distantly. "They were fighting next to one another. She was caught off-guard and Prince Marcus was preoccupied, fighting off several Rymidonians at once, unable to save her."

I had often wondered if I had not been locked away in the castle if I could have prevented the deaths of my brothers, of my father. If I could have saved Sakari from Skye's hand. Surely, if I'd been on that battlefield and had stood between them, they would've thought more clearly, would've thought through their actions.

I was foolish. I knew that. Skye and my father had been too far-gone to be saved, but Sakari … maybe. I fought against the intense jolt in my chest, the tears that wanted to flow freely.

"How do you know about Nerida?" Kai asked Lia. "I don't think I have seen him with a single soul. He's always alone."

Lia hesitated before she answered, "Nerida was a friend of mine. She wasn't a Royal. We shared a certain … connection. She loved Prince Marcus and he her, but they weren't allowed to bond because she wasn't a Royal. And from what I know, they weren't supposed to spend any time together in public, so as to not draw the attention of his father. Hence why you never saw them together. They did so behind King Ronan and Queen Aislinn's back."

So, the look in his eyes wasn't anger or somberness. It was sorrow, misery. He'd lost the woman he loved and he could show no one his grief. That was something I could understand. No one, not even myself, understood how I could mourn my father and Skye. I couldn't show my heartache for them. It would mean showing heartache for tyrants, traitors … murderers.

"He never approached me at the Awakening," Calliope said, reflective. "Every kingdom introduced themselves to me that night, trying to arrange a bonding, but I never once spoke with Marcus. She must've been why."

"She was," Lia said without reservation.

It must have been apparent that we were watching Prince Marcus, because his gaze cut to the five of us. I wanted to shy away from his stare, but I was fixed in place. The dark green of his irises intensified under the canopy of trees and foliage. My heart recognized something in him, latched onto the restrained pain in his eyes. Almost as quickly as he focused on us, he looked away.

"He'll probably leave without saying a word. Should I greet him? I mean…" Calliope looked at us uncertainly, "He's come to Faylinn a few times now, but we've never met. And I haven't really thanked him for saving me. I should do that," she decided. "Kai, will you stay with Lia and Cameron?"

He didn't appear pleased, but Kai agreed without protest.

"May I come with you?" I asked. "I'd also like to properly introduce myself. The more Royals I become acquainted with, the better I think I shall feel about Rymidon's positive transformation."

"Of course, yeah. Good idea. Let's go." Calliope offered her elbow, and we walked arm-in-arm toward the daunting man.

"Prince Marcus." Calliope prompted him to focus on us. His mouth set in a straight line, and his eyes narrowed, not as if he were angry, merely confused as to why we were approaching him. I was beginning to feel as though he kept his countenance as such to ward off conversation.

"Hi," Calliope greeted, extending her hand. His eyes drifted to her waiting hand, scrutinizing before he slowly wrapped his fingers around her wrist. "I wanted to welcome you to Faylinn and officially introduce myself."

He nodded curtly, but didn't say a word.

Calliope was undeterred. "This is Sarai of Rymidon. She became queen after The Battle."

When our eyes met, there was fire in his—a forest fire. I bowed my head. "Prince Marcus, it's a pleasure."

His brow lifted, but his facial expression remained the same—intense and skeptical. "I wasn't aware Adair had a daughter." The deep timbre of his voice amplified his stern face.

"You're not the only one." Calliope chuckled.

"Or rather, now that I think about it, it was rumored you'd died with your mother," he said.

Part of me wished to be locked away in my room once more; sealing myself from his brooding glare, but the queen in me lifted my chin and said, "My father kept me hidden for my protection after my mother was killed, or rather, as security that he'd always have an heir to the throne." He'd *claimed* protection, but I knew better now. However, this wasn't the time to air all his crimes.

Prince Marcus pressed his lips tightly and nodded once. "So, you're the only surviving member of your family?"

I kept my voice steady. "I am."

His eyes softened, turning the forest fire to pools of woe. "That must be difficult. My sympathies to you and your kingdom. I understand that Adair's Supremacy was quite strong."

It was more difficult than I'd imagined, hearing my father's name repeated in past tense. "I'm told he didn't give our kingdom much of a choice in many matters."

"Were you not under his Supremacy?"

"I didn't need to be, though I'm sure there were a few times. I conversed with very few fae and believed everything my father told me. I had no reason not to."

Prince Marcus subtly nodded, but said no more. His eyes never strayed from mine. They teetered between wary and captivated. Captivated by what, I wasn't sure.

My story *was* unusual. I imagined most kingdoms were confused by my claim to the throne, but I had grown up in the castle. I wasn't ignorant of how to rule Rymidon. What my father didn't teach me, Sakari provided. No one would be able to mark me as naïve or weak. I might have been inexperienced, but what I lacked in experience, I compensated for in compassion and loyalty and commitment. Rymidon wouldn't be spurned for long. I had every intention of rebuilding Rymidon and gaining every other kingdom's trust once more.

"I assure you, Prince Marcus, that Rymidon is not the kingdom it was when my father was king. If possible, I'd like to arrange a meeting with Oraelia, outside of this celebration, to reinstate our alliance. I know we have plenty to offer Oraelia in trade, weaponry, and security, among other things."

The corner of his mouth twitched before he rubbed his hand down his mouth and chin. Covering a smile? Or a laugh? "My father isn't here tonight, but I will speak with him and have his advisor contact Rymidon. That is all I can do."

Did he find me laughable? I attempted to keep lightness in my voice to remain civil, but his stance and expression led me to believe he wasn't taking me seriously. "Thank you."

"Well," Calliope exhaled. "Enough shop talk. Let's dance!" She waved Kai, Cameron, and Lia over.

I turned back to ask Prince Marcus if he would like to join us, but he'd disappeared. I scanned the meadow in hopes of catching him before he departed, but he was nowhere to be seen.

EIGHT

CAMERON

"If Calliope expects us to dance," Lia grumbled as we walked toward Callie, "I'm out."

"Party pooper."

"Where did he go?" Callie asked Sarai as we approached, looking beyond her shoulder.

"I don't know. When I turned around, he was gone."

"Dangit!" She flailed her arms like a child throwing a tantrum. "I was trying to get you two on the dance floor together."

Sarai looked startled. "What? Why?"

"He would be the perfect match for you."

Sarai exhaled loudly. "Calliope..."

"What? You will need to bond soon, won't you?"

"We've had more important things to worry about," Sarai suppressed her laughter, "but yes, I presume I'll need to in the near future."

"I'm free." I winked.

Sarai smiled, but I didn't think she took me seriously. Calliope's eyes shot daggers.

I raised my hands in surrender. "I was kidding." Partially.

Kai reached for Calliope to dance, distracting her. I took that as my opening to dance with Sarai. I took hold of her hand and spun her around to face me.

"Omph!" she huffed when her chest collided with mine. I hadn't meant to use so much force. I only wanted her close to me. With one arm around her waist, I took her hand in mine and spun us around the meadow. Her head tilted back as she laughed, carefree. It occurred to me that Sarai probably hadn't had any fun in quite some time.

"What is this dance?" She giggled.

"Huh?"

"Your way of dancing. What is it called?"

Uh. "I just call it dancing." We swayed from side-to-side. "How do you dance?"

Sarai's eyes twinkled, and her mouth upturned. Taking a step back, she untangled herself from me and twirled in a circle. Her right leg extended out rhythmically with the music as she gracefully swayed her arms in the air. Her deep purple dress whirled with every spin and twist. Sarai looked ethereal. I doubted I'd ever used that word before, but that was exactly the word to describe her. I could stand back and watch her dance all night. She was enchanting.

"Calliope will kill you," Lia's voice came over my shoulder.

I inhaled and swayed with the music. "I know."

"It would never work."

"I know." I exhaled.

"Then why do you insist on torturing yourself?"

My eyes shifted to Lia, and I smirked. "I guess I'm a masochist."

She rolled her eyes and sighed like I was the biggest idiot on the planet. I probably was. To my surprise, Lia danced away from me, like she couldn't help herself. Once she gained a bit of distance, she danced as if no one else were here. Not as much of a party pooper as I'd thought.

I watched Lia for a minute as her red hair swept across her face and her shoulders. She didn't make eye contact with a soul. She danced for herself. Everything around her faded, a spotlight shining on her. My eyes zeroed in. Her movements were subtler than Sarai's. Lia ignored everyone as she closed her eyes and let the music fuel her limbs.

A hand wrapped around mine, and I blinked, bringing my attention back to Sarai. Her teal eyes glimmered with laughter. For a brief second I'd forgotten about her. *What happened to me?*

I smiled, not looking back at Lia. "Where'd you learn to dance like that?"

"There wasn't much I could do in my room when I was alone, so I danced."

"A natural. It must be a faery thing."

It was difficult to tell in the dark, but it looked like Sarai was blushing. Ten points for Cameron.

Time was nonexistent in Faylinn. We could've been dancing for minutes, hours, or days, and I wouldn't have known the difference. I wanted to keep dancing. All night. Sarai was beautiful. The sky was unreal. Faylinn was nirvana. The faintest layer of fog settled over my mind. Before, it had taken more time in Faylinn to feel this way, but I already felt like I could stay forever and never miss the real world.

Calliope snatched my hand and dragged me out of the dancing crowd. I fought her at first, but it was pointless. She was so much stronger than me. I couldn't win.

She placed a hand on either side of my face and examined my eyes. "Are you okay?"

"Yeah, I'm great," I said, smiling. "Why?"

"You've got a glassy look in your eyes. I don't like it."

I snorted, brushing her hands aside. "You're too worried. I'm fine. Perfectly sane."

"Where do you go to school?"

I laughed. "Clemson."

"Where were you born?"

"Walhalla," I said with an eye roll.

"What are your roommates' names?"

I blink once. Twice.

"Cameron," she hissed.

I shook my head and cleared my throat. "Chase and Ryland." That was weird.

She sighed. "Okay. I think we should get you out of here sooner than later. Maybe coming to Faylinn isn't the best idea."

"Sure it is. We're having fun."

"I'm going to put a Keeper on guard in the forest near your apartments, so if you need to get in touch with me, you'll be able to."

"That seems a little excessive, don't you think, Cal?"

"Not when my best friend is a human. I want you to be able to stay in touch in case of an emergency. I should've done that in the first place. I hate being out of the loop." She continued to examine my pupils. "Did you eat anything? Drink anything?"

"What, is this Wonderland?" I chuckled. "If I eat a cookie, will I grow into a giant? Or if I eat a mushroom will I shrink?"

"It's not funny, Cam. Did you feel like this the last time you were here and just didn't tell me?"

"Callie. I'm. Fine. And I'm pretty sure last time the circumstances were a little different. I had fear and sheer desire to survive driving me before."

Sarai approached us. Hours must have passed while we danced, but Sarai didn't even look winded. Not a single drop of sweat. "Is everything all right?"

"Yeah, I just want to get Cameron back home. I forgot the effect fae music has on humans. He'd never stop dancing if I didn't make him."

"Oh." A frown formed on her lips. Was she disappointed I had to leave? "Well, before you take him home, I was hoping I could have a moment in private with you, Calliope."

"Yes, of course. But first, where is Lia?" We searched the dancing faeries until I spotted her still in her own world, weaving in and out of the crowd, her face to the sky as she twirled.

"I'll go get her," I said.

"Oh, no you don't." Calliope stopped me. "Kai, will you get Lia and stay with her and Cameron while I speak with Sarai? And don't let them dance anymore."

He rolled his eyes, but it seemed to be aimed at Lia, not Calliope. He marched out to get Lia, while I waited.

"Declan, could you escort Sarai and me to the atrium?"

"Yes, My Queen." Declan appeared out of nowhere. *Sneaky son of a gun.*

"Declan," Calliope groaned.

"Where'd you come from?" I asked.

"Where have you been?" Calliope's eyebrow rose, questioning me. "Declan's my personal Keeper. He's been here the whole night."

My focus might have been captivated by someone a little more *my* speed. Kai was walking our way with Lia in tow. I gradually noticed faeries stepping aside, making room for her. Not to be polite, but as if she were a disease they didn't want to catch.

"Well," I cleared my throat and brought my attention back to Calliope, "he sure is stealthy."

"Then I'm doing my job right." Declan nodded at me and swept his hand in front of his frame so Calliope and Sarai would pass. You'd think I'd be used to Calliope as royalty by now, but as she walked away with Declan and a few other Keepers trailing behind her, scoping the joint, I couldn't hold back my chuckle.

"What's so funny?" Kai asked.

"She's a queen."

He looked at me like he wanted to admit me to a psych ward. Maybe he should. I'm in a magical faery land. My best friend is a faery queen. I have a crush on another faery queen who can never be mine. And my temporary roommate happens to be a faery turned human. I'm surrounded by faeries. *How is this my life?*

"I just have to remind myself sometimes."

"Sometimes I have to remind myself that she's mine." Kai's voice was so soft, he probably didn't think I'd heard him. His eyes stayed fixed on her until she disappeared behind the castle gates.

Castle. I laughed to myself again. She lived there. I shook my head and pulled my attention back to the faeries chatting and dancing in the meadow.

"Are we leaving soon?" Lia sighed. "This music is going to kill me if we don't leave soon."

"Sarai needed to talk to Calliope first, but then we can go." Lia and I began to sway with the music. Kai grabbed each of our elbows and escorted us forward. "Maybe we should wait inside the castle."

With her arms folded across her chest, Lia let her eyes drift over the castle grounds. *What's she thinking about? Scratch that.* There was only one thing she could be thinking about, or rather, someone.

To distract her, I said, "I have a feeling I'm going to be late to school in the morning."

"What's one missed test when you get to spend the weekend in Faylinn?" She shrugged.

"How did you know I was going to miss a test?"

"It's like you think I never listen."

"That's because I didn't think you did."

"There's a lot that you assume about me, Cameron."

NINE

SARAI

With a heavy sigh, Calliope fell back onto the window seat in the atrium. "Oh, Sarai, that's horrible. You shouldn't have to deal with something like this right now."

"My main concern is what they want with the blood, or if it serves a purpose for them at all."

Calliope scratched her temple. "This might be a stupid question, but why would anyone want to drain our blood?"

I forget how little she knew and was still learning. "It's the source of our powers: the healing, the elements, enticement, cultivating nature, everything."

"Yeah, but how could it be used by anyone except for us? Could it be used against us?"

"It's possible. I've never known this to happen before. I don't even know if our blood could benefit anyone else or if it's powerless without our bodies as a vessel. We've always lived in peace with the other beings. If my family were still alive, I'd ask one of them all of these questions, but I don't want to cause unnecessary concern or distress by asking around Rymidon. I don't know who else to turn to."

"You came to the right place. I'll find out what I can," she said reassuringly, standing up. "I have plenty of resources to ask that I trust to be discreet."

"Thank you, Calliope. I knew I'd be able to trust in you."

"Sarai, always." She took my hand firmly in her grasp. "We're family. I still consider you my sister. I always will."

Holding back tears, I kept my resilient appearance and hugged Calliope. "As I you."

"I still miss him," she whispered, clinging tighter to me.

Sakari bound us together forever. I choked on tears. "Me too."

TEN

CAMERON

"Well, that party wasn't nearly as exciting as I hoped it'd be. Is it just me or has the faery scene lost all the action? Not to mention, Calliope was a buzzkill."

Lia didn't respond as we walked from the forest through the parking lot to my apartment. I thought I'd at least get a grunt or scowl of some sort, but there was nothing.

"No one showed up unwelcome. No one attacked Faylinn. No one was kidnapped or murdered. I'm a little disappointed."

She stared straightforward, not even a twitch to her lips as I pulled stray leaves and twigs from my hair.

"And here we are arriving at," I flash the screen on my cell phone since I turned it back on, "two AM and I feel like I could sleep for a week. I think Faylinn shaves off more than time. Did I age? I've gotta be up at seven for my exam. On less than five hours of sleep, I'm probably screwed."

"You poor baby." *Finally.*

"It's a rough life, but who else can say they spent the weekend with a bunch of mystical creatures?"

"Me." Her voice remained monotone.

For some reason, I needed more of a reaction out of her. She was so reserved in Faylinn until she danced. I knew it was hard for her to be there, but I figured it would've helped her attitude a little bit. Something told me it didn't.

I tossed out the first thing my brain could think of to grab her attention. "Chase is going to ask you out."

"Who?"

I stopped. *She's joking right?* "My roommate, Chase."

Her eyes bunched together. I couldn't tell if Lia was confused or disgusted. "Is he the quiet one or the one who thinks he's God's gift to women?" She's been living with us for months. How did she not know which one he was?

I snorted. "The latter."

Her top lip curled up. Disgust. Definitely disgust. "Ugh. No, thank you."

"I figured you'd say as much, but nothing I said was going to deter him."

Lia gave me a side-glance before walking up the stairwell. "You tried to deter him?"

"No way." I laughed, following behind her as we climbed the stairs of my apartment building. "I'm going to get a front row seat to you rejecting him."

"We'll see about that."

"Are you saying you're not going to reject him?"

"I didn't say that."

I turned the lock on the apartment door and looked over

my shoulder. "So, you *are* going to tell him no."

"I didn't say that either."

"Just a minute ago you were repulsed by the thought of him asking you out."

"Maybe I changed my mind."

I chuckled and shook my head as I opened the door. "Suit yourself."

"Where have *you* two been all weekend?"

"Chase." I startled, gripping the doorknob to steady myself.

Lia gasped and crouched into a defensive pose, like a feral animal ready to lunge. *Down, girl.*

Chase sat at our kitchen table under dim lighting, eating a bowl of cereal.

"You scared the tar out of us."

"Sorry, bro." He laughed. "I thought you saw me." His head tilted to the side with an eyebrow raised, assessing Lia. She quickly straightened up.

"What are you still doing up?" I asked to cover up Lia's strange behavior.

He paused before he answered, "Late night snack, then I'm heading to bed. But seriously, where have you guys been? I left the apartment for like five minutes on Friday, and when I got back y'all were gone. I figured you'd leave a note or something if you weren't going to be here all weekend."

"Sorry, Mom. We went and hung out at Callie's place for the weekend."

"Who?"

"Callie. She was here on Friday. Blonde curly hair, big green—"

Lia elbowed me in the ribs. "Ow!" My ribs were taking a

beating tonight.

"You must be smoking crack." Chase snorted as he dropped his empty bowl in the sink. "You never introduced me to anyone."

Crap. What was I thinking? Of course he didn't remember meeting her on Friday. Faery magic and all. "I must've introduced her to Ryland."

"Well, it definitely wasn't me. Is she hot?"

"She's married."

"Bummer. You seem to have good taste in female friends." Chase's eyes scaled Lia up and down. A weird feeling of protectiveness overcame me, which made no sense. I've watched Chase check out a million different girls, and I'd only known him a few months. What did I care if he had a thing for Lia? She *was* attractive. It didn't change the fact that she was a cold-hearted snake.

"Well, I'm going to bed. I'm only going to get like four hours of sleep as it is." I looked to Lia. "You good?"

She gave me a funny look. What was wrong with making sure she was comfortable staying alone with Chase? "I'm fine," she snapped.

Realization hit me. I've never cared to ask about her wellbeing before. "Right. Well. Night, guys."

ELEVEN

LIA

"Night bro." Chase gave Cameron a head nod, and then proceeded to take off his shirt as he walked out of the kitchen, hovering in front of the hallway. He draped his T-shirt around the back of his neck and smiled at me. If he knew I'd spent my entire life around shirtless men with bodies a million times more fit than his, he might not feel so confident walking around with his wannabe six-pack beer belly.

Turning my back on him, I moved to set up my bed on the couch in the living room. I'd managed to avoid Chase for this long and had no intention of breaking the streak any time soon.

"You and Cam have a good weekend?"

Why was he talking to me? "Sure."

"What did y'all do?"

Was it just me or was he prying? How would he react if I

told him the truth? I laughed to myself. I almost told just to see his reaction. Maybe he'd think I was crazy and leave me alone. "We just hung out."

He laughed, deep and quiet. Did I say something funny? "You're very cryptic. I dig it."

When I'd talked to Cameron, I knew I'd made it seem like I wouldn't reject Chase, but the more he talked, the more I wanted to gag Chase with the T-shirt hanging around his neck.

"You free tomorrow night?" He hovered by the armrest as I laid out the sheet and blanket Cameron had given me to make my bed.

Did I appear remotely interested? Was my blatant lack of eye contact and curt answers begging for his attention? Maybe he needed a clingy girl to deter him. Too bad I couldn't muster up the acting chops it would take for that façade.

I finally looked up when I tossed down my pillow. "Not for you."

"Oh, harsh." He chuckled, pretending to be wounded. His hand clung to his chest. "Mysterious, beautiful, *and* hard to get." Chase clicked his tongue and swiped it across his bottom lip. Was that supposed to sexy? I, in no way, found him appealing. If anything, I was more repulsed. "All right. I can take a hint." His self-assured smile never faded. *Cocky little bugger.*

I walked past him to wash my face and brush my teeth in the bathroom at the end of the hall. He followed close on my heels.

"If you change your mind, you know where to find me." *Can take a hint, my butt.*

"It's unlikely, but thanks." I closed the bathroom door in his face.

TWELVE

CAMERON

The bathroom door clicked shut, and it took every part of me to keep from laughing out loud. I should've taken the opportunity to go to sleep, but when I'd heard Chase coming onto Lia as I was closing my bedroom door I *had* to listen to the rest of the conversation.

If I'd been around when he'd asked, she might've said yes just to prove me wrong, but I knew she didn't want to. It felt good to know I'd been right. She didn't want to say yes to Chase. I mean … Skye was too fresh in her mind. It seemed to me, she was too closed off to ever love someone again. We might not talk much, but I've had enough time over the last few months to observe her. She wouldn't bother giving someone like Chase the time of day. It would take an army to break down the guard she's built around her heart.

When I left for my exam after 6:30 AM, I wasn't surprised to see Lia sound asleep. Her hair splayed like fire licking across her cheek, the sunlight streaming through the blinds. I stopped to watch her. She looked like a different person when she slept, so serene and untouched by the world. Then I realized how creepy it would look if she woke up, or Ryland or Chase found me staring, and darted toward the front door. I nearly slammed it on my way out, but thought better of it before shutting it quietly.

Maybe when I was done with my exam and classes, Lia and I could go together to find her a job. She wasn't going to find one without me, and the sooner I found her a position, the sooner I'd have her out of my hair.

That is what I wanted, wasn't it?

"What are you doing?" Lia looked at me the way the most popular girl in school looked at the outcast, when I sat down beside her on the couch with my laptop in hand later that night.

"C'mon. We're gonna take a look at job listings. There's got to be a restaurant that needs a hostess or server or something. I feel like restaurants are always hiring. And in a college town—"

She groaned, hitting mute on the TV remote. "I told you I've been trying."

"I know, but I figured a little help couldn't hurt. Maybe with our powers combined we'll find something."

"Do you think we can find a place that pays under the table? Even with my fake ID, the government has no record of me for payroll and such."

Hmm … I didn't think of that. "We'll figure something out."

I felt her fidgeting beside me and looked over to see Lia looking at the screen, threading a reddish-orange ribbon between her fingers, rubbing it wordlessly as I scrolled through the classifieds.

"What are you doing with that?"

"Huh?" I nodded toward the ribbon in her hand. "Oh … it reminds me of the texture of my wings." Her voice was so quiet I could barely hear her. Music streamed from the hallway, reminding me Ryland was back there studying. She must've been concerned he'd hear her. His music was loud enough that I knew he couldn't.

Lia shrugged. "Same color, too."

"Oh yeah, I remember. You had uh, really cool wings."

The first time I saw Lia as a faery in Faylinn, I'd thought I was hallucinating. It had been the most bizarre scene. Her wings were like flames sprouting from her back, commanding attention without so much as a word. Had I not hated her in that moment, I might have been drawn to her. "Is that what you miss the most?"

I heard her soft sigh. "Yeah."

My dad had once told me it helped to talk about my problems and feelings rather than keeping them bottled up. Ironic, considering he'd never talked about his problems, so I'd never talked about mine. It was a shaky ground to cross with

Lia, but I decided to do it anyway. "What do you miss most about them?"

"Are you seriously asking me about my wings?" She said 'wings' like she was telling me a secret.

"Yeah. Why not? Calliope said they don't serve much of a purpose, that they're essentially a gender differentiation feature, but there has to be more to it than that if you miss them that much."

Lia peered at me to see if I was serious. I stared back, waiting. Talking about faery stuff and Faylinn was so much more interesting than talking about the real world. It was a miracle I didn't spiral into some crazy depression after coming back the first time and being thrown straight into homework and studying and major declarations. It was all so monotonous and boring.

When Calliope had left to rule the faery world, it was easy to forget what I knew about her and live a normal life when she wasn't constantly around. But I'd never seen the other side. However, now that Lia was with me all the time, nothing faded. I remembered everything. In detail. There were some things I wished could be wiped from my mind completely, like the memory of the battlefield aftermath and the sounds of terror and cries Kai and I could hear from that burrow. But, ultimately, I didn't want to forget. The fantasy realm brought vibrancy and magic to my otherwise mundane life.

Lia drew her attention back to my computer and took control of scrolling. "Did you ever have a favorite stuffed animal you slept with when you were little? Or a blanket? Anything?"

I chuckled to myself. "When I was eight, I had a Superman action figure. For years, he stood on my nightstand to watch the night and protect me. When my mom left, he served as a companion so I never felt alone again." Where did that come from? My mom was a topic I never talked about. I didn't think Callie even knew about Superman.

Lia's eyes flashed the briefest sadness before she covered it up and said, "Well, picture Superman like an appendage. No matter where you were or what you were doing, he was there to comfort you or alert you to something awry. He could react to things quicker than your brain or your heart, an instinct. He could wrap his arms around you and comfort you when you were sad, and commiserate with any pain. Superman was the best friend who never needed to talk, an internal communication only the two of you understood."

She broke eye contact. I knew she was no longer diligently searching for a job listing, but Lia still scrolled down the screen. "Now, imagine being your eight-year-old self and Superman was stolen. You could never get him back. You were left to fend for yourself alone in the dark. He was no longer there to shield you from the things that go bump in the night or be your companion. You no longer had your security. All you have is yourself."

I watched her profile while she tried to appear unaffected. Her jaw twitched, and she blinked rapidly. Quickly, she swiped her hand under her eye, as if she were being discreet.

"That really sucks."

She shrugged and nodded. "I'm adapting."

To me, she wanted to sound like a tough girl, but the fragile facade was cracking. She couldn't keep up the indifferent act much longer. Part of me wanted to shatter the pretenses to get to what was underneath all the attitude and bitterness. Another part of me clung to my animosity and disinterest. The sooner she was gone, the better.

I kept saying that, and yet, it was getting more and more difficult to believe it.

THIRTEEN

SARAI

"Your Highness."

I gasped awake, shooting straight up from my pillow. The blanket pooled around my waist. I blinked, my eyes adjusting to the dark and my intruder.

"I'm sorry to disturb you." Kayne came into view, hovering in my open chamber doorway. He peered over his lean shoulder and then closed the door behind him, cloaking us in darkness. With a sweep of my arm, candles lit around the room. "You wanted me to come to you as soon as possible if more came to light in regards to the assassinations." He turned his back to me when my state of undress struck him.

Quickly, I got out of bed and wrapped a robe around my thin nightgown. "Yes, what is it, Kayne?"

He peeked over his shoulder to make sure I was decent before turning all the way around. "Another was found. Throat slashed, blood drained, body dumped in the forest just outside the kingdom walls."

"Who?"

"Sindri of the Craftsmen."

"Odila's son." My heart weighed in my chest. "So, they aren't targeting one colony."

"No, Your Grace."

"Has Calliope contacted us since the uniting celebration?" His head shook once. "No, Your Grace."

It had been days. I sighed. "And there was still no evidence around the body? Nothing to tie him to where he was killed or by whom?"

Kayne lowered his voice. "No, Your Grace." I could tell his lack of useful information disheartened him.

Staring up at the wooden beams on the tall ceiling, I held in my tears. I wouldn't cry in front of Kayne. He needed to see my strength, not flailing for answers.

With a heavy exhale I looked at him. "Thank you for waking me and letting me know. We'll come together first thing. I want a meeting with you and the Keepers who found Sindri and the Keepers who found Eldon."

"Yes, Your Highness."

"Thank you, Kayne. You may go now," I dismissed him before he could see my weakness.

There was hesitation before he bowed and backed out of my chambers.

My legs instantly collapsed beneath me and tears took control. I missed Sakari. I missed him so much. I missed his strength and advice. I missed his comfort and tenacity. He would've known precisely what to do. Why couldn't he have lived, and I'd have died? Rymidon would've been better off in his capable hands. All I could do was sit back and wait for another assassination and hope we'd have more answers next time. Soon, I wouldn't be able to hide this. Soon, the entire kingdom would know we were being hunted one by one and there was nothing their queen could do for them.

Oh, Sakari. Why did you have to leave me?

"The bodies are placed in the same position when they're found. On their backs with their hands crossed over their chests."

"Almost in a respectful manner," I concluded.

"Yes, Your Highness," Brae answered.

"Is there anything else you can tell me about their bodies? Any other marks or cuts?"

"No, Your Highness. No bruising. No other wounds. Only the slit across the throat."

"So, we can assume they aren't being tortured. Their deaths are quick."

Brae nodded. "I would say that is a safe assumption. From what we have gathered after examining the bodies, it doesn't look as if they protected themselves. So, either Eldon and Sindri knew the assassin, they were caught by surprise, or their arms were secured to keep them from fighting back."

The doors of the hall flew open—slamming against the walls—and in walked a very menacing looking Marcus of Oraelia. His burly figure filled the room, his eyes ablaze.

"Your Highness," Galdinon rushed in behind him, "I'm sorry. I couldn't stop him. I tried."

"It's quite all right, Galdinon." I stood at the head of the table. "Prince Marcus, is there something I can do for you?"

"Was the Battle of Faylinn not enough for you?"

Brae, Gallagher, Eitri, and Kayne stood and closed in to shield me.

"Excuse me?"

His fury gushed out of him in a surge. "I have two dead Keepers on my hands, and I can't think of any other kingdom who would find it necessary to slit the throats of our own kind. Were you attempting to get our attention? Reclaim your dominance? Show your power? As the daughter of Adair I can't say I'm surprised."

His accusation caused me to stand taller and narrow my eyes. "Prince Marcus, while I understand that you are upset, and our kingdom may seem to be the likely enemy at this time, please have more decency than to come into *my* kingdom and accuse *me* of such an act before considering more facts."

Prince Marcus lifted one long finger and jabbed it in my direction. "Are you denying your hand in it?" The volume of his voice never lowered, booming off the stone walls.

"If it is one of my own, it was not under my direction." I placed my palms flat on the table and leveled my stare. "So, if you would be so kind as to lower your finger and give me the respect I deserve in my own castle, maybe then we can converse like civilized beings."

The anger in Prince Marcus's eyes minimally dissipated. He blinked, grunting his consent, and lowered his hand.

"Kayne," I murmured, "May Prince Marcus and I have the room."

"My Queen, are you sure?"

I nodded once. "I will be fine."

"I do not feel comfortable with this, but as you wish."

The rest of the Keepers followed Kayne single-file out of the gathering hall and closed the door, giving us privacy.

"My council and I were just discussing the recent assassinations on our grounds. So, it seems to me we have a common enemy."

Prince Marcus drew closer, minding his steps around the table as he walked down the long hall to meet me. "Were your faeries' throats slashed?"

"Yes. With no indication of the murder around the body?" I questioned him.

He nodded his head curtly.

"We've found two of our own in the forest within the last moon cycle, and I fear they will not be the last."

"Do you have any idea as to who may be behind the killings?" he asked.

"We're attempting to narrow down the possibilities, but unfortunately, we don't have much to go on. I cannot say with certainty it wasn't a Rymidonian. As of right now, it is not my suspicion, but I am not ruling it out."

His shoulders relaxed, and he pointed toward a chair closest to mine, asking with his eyes if he may have a seat.

"Please." I gestured and took my seat.

"Forgive me, Queen Sarai." He lowered his head as he sat and rested his clasped hands on the tabletop. "I believe the Battle of Faylinn has taken a toll on us, and I did not think before I acted. I hope you can forgive my intrusion."

"There is nothing to forgive. I understand what my father did, and I am fully aware that it will take time for our kingdom to be trusted. If I were in your position I cannot say I wouldn't have done the same thing. When you are responsible for so many, the desire to protect intensifies."

A hint of a smile lit his eyes. "Yes. It does."

He had very nice eyes when they weren't set on killing me. Shaking my head, I cleared the thought before I spoke. "Well, maybe our kingdoms can come together and pool our resources to catch the assassin."

"I think that would be wise."

"I will say I am surprised it was you who stormed my castle." I kept the teasing in my voice. "King Ronan seems like the type to take matters into his own hands."

"He is. He wanted to invade Rymidon with an army. I convinced him to let me come and speak to you first, before we made any hasty decisions."

Oh. "Well, then I suppose I should be giving you my thanks."

"How about we call it equal?" A full smile graced his face, and the strangest thing happened to my stomach. It felt like it was soaring through the trees, fluttering and light.

I smiled in return. "I agree to that."

"Good." Prince Marcus held my gaze. "I will return to Oraelia and speak with my father. It would be wise to contact the other kingdoms to see if any of them have lost anyone."

"I will have Kayne begin the communication."

"And I will also, so they are aware you aren't the only ones being targeted. If we work together, hopefully we'll get to the bottom of this quickly and efficiently."

"I now have faith it is possible." There was something about Prince Marcus, something trustworthy, and I was in desperate need of more fae I could depend on.

"Well." He stood and glanced falteringly around the room. "I believe time is valuable at this point, so I should be on my way."

I stood. "Thank you, Prince Marcus."

"Please, you may call me Marcus. No need to carry on with formalities." His tone was lighter, almost toying with me. I could feel my cheeks flush with heat.

"Oh. Okay. Well, thank you ... Marcus." I tasted his name on my lips. It was surprising how much I enjoyed it.

He nodded with a faint side-smile. "We'll be in touch."

FOURTEEN

LIA

No one needed to give me a run down of Skye's offenses. I knew them well. Hearing them out loud only made me hate Skye. And I didn't want to hate him. I could hate the corruption he'd fallen for, and the horrible acts he'd carried out, but not him. Never him.

Being in Faylinn had solidified that. I couldn't get the words out of my head. Everywhere I'd turned, the moment someone saw me, there were choruses about how pathetic I was to love a monster like Skye. Did they think my human ears couldn't hear them? Surely not. They'd wanted me to know how disgusting I was, had wanted to me to drown in the miserable life I'd created for myself.

I hated Adair. I hated the way his Supremacy soaked into Skye and poisoned everything good that was left of him. Brainwashed him until there was nothing left of the Skye I loved.

I rubbed the ribbon, weaving it between my fingers—my security blanket—and watched the rain trickle down the front windows.

Wished and wanted weren't strong enough words to describe how desperately I wanted to go back and change what had happened. Yearned? Craved? Ached? Everything combined. If I knew then what I know now … Oh, the things I could have done differently.

I couldn't say I regretted making the deal with Adair to come to this world and get to know Calliope. She was the only good thing I'd gotten out of this mess, but that had been the first act to set things in motion. Though, had I said no, Adair would've found another way. If I hadn't been the catalyst, someone else would have been. So, as much as I wished I hadn't been the one to give Adair insight, I couldn't regret it. Without it, I might not even have Calliope as an ally now.

However, when I'd returned to Rymidon before we'd invaded Faylinn, I would've somehow tried to convince Skye to run away with me. I would've done everything in my power to counteract Adair's Supremacy. And if that hadn't worked, I would've kidnapped Skye, made him see the wrong of his ways, away from Adair's control. If I could've been strong enough, wise enough—more persistent—maybe Skye would've listened to me. If I'd had a backbone, maybe he'd still be alive. Maybe everyone who lost their life would still be alive.

If it weren't for me.

FIFTEEN

CAMERON

When I walked out into the main room of my apartment to grab a glass of water before bed, I noticed Lia sitting in the dark near the windows overlooking the parking lot and forest beyond. Rain pelted the glass. It was a calming site. Made me want to watch the rain with her, which was a strange thought.

Lia didn't turn or acknowledge the fact that I'd walked into the room. Her back remained straight, her figure motionless. She hadn't heard me come in. I should've turned away and given her privacy. Then I heard a sniffle.

Without thought, I asked, "You okay?"

"Huh?" Lia swiftly wiped her hands across her cheeks. *Are those tears? Does Soul Sucker have a heart?*

"I said, are you okay?" I walked closer.

"I'm fine." Her voice was short, unyielding. She wouldn't meet me in the eye. If anything, she angled herself further away from me. "Why?"

"You want to talk about it?" I asked, sitting down on the armrest closest to her.

She cleared her throat. "Talk about what?"

I thought carefully about what I wanted to say to her. "Well, I've been doing a lot of thinking…"

"That's a first," she snorted.

I decided to let her have that one. "As I was saying … I've been doing a lot of thinking, and I realized I've been a little tough on you. Not to say you don't deserve it. You made your bed, you've gotta sleep in it now."

"Do you have a point, Cameron?" she interrupted, slicing her eyes to me. While she was no longer a faery, her eyes were still a vivid hazel, nearly glowing in the dark. It was kind of terrifying. But in a weird, good way. In a way I wasn't quite ready to explore. Under the moonlight streaming through the window, I could see the sheen of tears glossing her red eyes under puffy eyelids. Maybe I should've been a little more sensitive.

"I know what you did for Callie—trading places with Kai—wasn't easy. There wasn't anything in it for you. It was pretty selfless, which was really big of you. And now you're stuck here. Not to mention you lost people, too."

"Not people. Just one." She turned away again. Her voice was so small I almost didn't understand her. I wasn't sure she wanted me to. It wasn't hard to figure out she was talking about King Evil, Jr. Whatever his name was.

"What did you see in that guy, anyway?"

She took a deep breath as she stared out the window. "Skye wasn't always so confused." Her tone was defensive.

"Confused?" I scoffed before I could hold back. "You

call him *confused*? He kidnapped me, *killed* Sakari. He tried to kill Calliope's dad. The man was downright delusional to think following his father was the right thing to do, and you want to call him *confused*?"

Her jaw clenched. Silence occupied the space between us.

"I know defending him to you will be pointless, but Skye loved me," she murmured. "He was good to me. He always had been. I might've been the only person he was good to, but it was enough." She took a deep breath. "I just think our *forbidden* love got the better of him. He would have done anything to be with me, and I for him. For so long we'd fought for our love, and Adair had used it against us. Saw a way to exploit it and make it work in his favor. All we saw was a way out, a way to be together, and nothing else mattered. It's truly crazy how love can make you blind. That's a human term I understand completely. When he gave me the option to spy on a human in exchange to bond with Skye, it seemed like the easiest thing Adair could've asked of me."

I kept quiet, afraid if I said anything, she'd clam up. She was finally opening up to me, and I wanted to hear everything she had to say.

"It wasn't until Rymidon took over Faylinn that I saw what I'd done, what I'd set in motion. Adair never gave me much information on his plans. All I knew was that I was supposed to give him information on Calliope, anything strange about her and her life. I didn't know what he was going to do with it. Not at first. Not that it would have mattered in the beginning anyway. She was just another human to me. I didn't know she was a True Royal. I didn't even know she was a faery until she showed me her wings. I mean … I knew she had to be special enough for me to spy on, but he didn't trust me enough to tell me anything. His questions were always cryptic.

"Once I understood the magnitude of my actions, I was in too far." I saw tears pool in the corners of Lia's eyes. She blinked them away before I could wipe them for her. "I was so ashamed, and, if I'm being honest with myself, prideful. I didn't want to accept that I was wrong. I couldn't face Calliope because everything she had to say to me was true. And I was so blinded by my love for Skye, nothing else mattered except for the fact that I was *finally* able to be with him freely, without consequence. I kept telling myself it was worth it. Little did I know there were consequences. Consequences of gigantic proportion, but there was nothing I could do to stop it. Adair was my king, and therefore—because I was a faery again—I had to follow him, honor him, and obey him. His Supremacy would've forced me to if I hadn't. He gave me Skye, and at the time, I thought that was all I needed."

Lia paused. I thought she was finished until she quietly said, "Regrettably, it wasn't until I saw Skye send an arrow into Sakari's heart that I realized how far gone he was. He was willing to kill his own brother to see his father's plan through. I wanted to believe that my Skye was still in there. That we just needed to get through this hurdle in order for him to come back to me, but in that moment before he was killed, I realized, I'd already lost him. I was never going to get him back, not even if we survived the war."

After a trembling breath, she blinked and added, "No matter what I do, I can't unlove him."

There were always two sides to every story. Calliope's was the only side I'd ever cared about before. It wasn't until now that I realized Lia had one, too—that I cared about her side.

And somewhere buried deep inside her chest was a beating heart. She was manipulated and used, betrayed and broken-hearted. Her choices were wrong, and she was going to deal with the guilt of her actions forever, but now at least I understood them. At least she was trying to make things right.

More tears fell from her shimmering eyes before she could stop them. I had the most bizarre urge to wipe them from her face and hold her, but I held back.

"I'm sorry."

She broke her gaze with the rain streaming down the windowpane. "For what?"

"I hate what you felt you needed to do, what you've had to endure to get here. I'm sorry you were placed in the position you were."

She snorted and looked down at her hands twisted in her lap. "It's my own doing, Cameron. No one to blame but myself."

"I think we can blame Adair a little bit."

Lia chuckled, and, for the first time it wasn't sardonic or mocking. She offered me a smile that finally reached her hazel eyes. "Umm … I haven't thanked you. I really do appreciate you taking me in, even if you only did it because Calliope asked you. You didn't have to, so thank you for taking pity on me."

"Honestly, I was terrified of Calliope's wrath," I joked.

"That little blonde thing can be quite terrifying."

"I'm sure you've seen more of that than I have." I laughed. "She was probably pretty bad-A on the battlefield, huh?"

Lia annunciated every word. "She was fierce."

SIXTEEN

SARAI

"I have good news, and I have bad news. What would you like to hear first?"

My heart couldn't handle anymore whiplash. "I have had enough bad news to last for an eternity. I need something good, Calliope. Please."

Her hands clapped together. "Okay. Well, it's not necessarily *good* news as much as it is useful information. I don't know who is behind the assassinations, but I have an idea as to why they are taking our blood."

"Should I have a seat for this?" I asked.

Calliope took my hands and guided us toward the window seat in my chamber. "There are scrolls documenting rulings and history that were created by my family after the Great Divide. All of them are supposed to be kept safe in the atrium in Faylinn for the eyes of the True Royals only. When I asked

Evan about our blood he said the scrolls would tell me. I've scoured them, Sarai and there's nothing. So, Evan counted them. Sure enough, I'm missing one."

"Where would it be?"

"Adair is the only one I know who had access to the atrium. I believe he stole the scroll and either it's somewhere hidden in Rymidon or he traded it or the information on it and our enemy now has it."

"I don't know where he would have hidden something like that. It could be anywhere. What's documented on this scroll?"

"From what Evan told me, it should detail all the powers our blood possesses, certain powers only a True Royal would or should know about. And, if in the wrong hands, the information could be life-threatening. It makes me wonder if they're using our blood to try to access our powers."

My stomach churned. I was going to be sick. "This does not narrow down our possible enemies," I said. "I'd imagine a considerable amount of beings in our world would kill to have our abilities if it were possible."

Calliope frowned. "That's the bad news. There's no way to know who wants our blood or for what purpose. Kai and I bounced around some ideas, trying to get in the mindset of the enemy. If they've attacked you and Oraelia, it's only a matter of time before Faylinn and the others are hit. Are they creating an army? Is it possible our blood creates enhanced warriors? Ones with immeasurable strength and skill. Ones with heightened abilities and size." A chill ran through my wings. "Or they could be creating monsters, for all we know. It may not give them our abilities at all, but have an aversion to our blood."

The chill seeped into my blood. "So we might not even be

dealing with normal faeries, but rabid beasts."

Calliope nodded gravely. "As I witnessed in the Battle of Faylinn, our powers aren't always sourced for good. We can be massively destructive. Our powers in the wrong hands…"

"Could potentially be the end of our race as we know it."

"Well, that escalated quickly."

I snorted out laughter. "Just imagining worst-case scenarios to prepare myself."

"Well, how about we remain optimistic and narrow down our enemies. What about the elves? I know they have a vendetta against Rymidon. I met Guthron the night of the Oak's awakening celebration and he was *not* pleasant. Quite frightening actually. Have you seen an elf in real life? Those teeth." She shivered.

I shook my head. "But Rymidon isn't the only target. The elves have no reason to attack us all. While these casualties don't add up to the Battle of Faylinn casualties, it's too many."

"Which is exactly why we need to question everyone; every being in every domain. We can't rule out a group simply because it doesn't make sense."

"You are right. It's as though you are Queen of Faylinn or something."

She smirked. "I've had a little practice."

"I have lost my ability to think." I swallowed, attempting to push down my unease. "I don't know what I'm doing, Calliope. Instinct took over initially, a near excitement for the future of Rymidon and the possibilities, but I fear I've lost it. I miss my family. I miss Sakari." At the mention of his name, her eyes grew sorrowful. "Being Queen of Rymidon has drained all of my optimism. How do you do it?"

"Listen, Sarai." Calliope placed her hands on top of mine.

"You're stronger, more determined, and smarter than I was when I was pulled into all of this. If I didn't have Declan and Kai and Allura and … Sakari, I wouldn't have made it out alive. I was thrown into this world practically blindfolded, bound, and gagged. I dealt with my fair share of enemies over the last year, but if I even had half the sense and heart that you do, I think Faylinn and I could've avoided a lot of pain and heartbreak. Forget your insecurities. You were born to rule. And you're not alone. You have me and loyal Keepers and Prince Marcus, from what I understand."

I couldn't stop the heat from rising to the surface of my cheeks. My eyes shied away from Calliope.

"I knew it!"

I shook my head and wanted to find a burrow to hide in.

"Stop shaking your head. You guys are MFEO."

"MF-what?"

"It's a human thing, from one of my favorite movies. You're meant for each other, so stop fighting it."

"We have been a little busy trying to save our kingdoms, Calliope. And he is still mourning Nerida. I doubt I have even crossed his mind in that way. Goodness, he just stormed into my castle and accused me of killing Oraelians. I doubt love or bonding are on his mind."

"Oh, stop. You two will get it figured out. Take it from a girl who was too stubborn to see a good thing in front of her the first time around … don't waste a day. As cliché as it sounds, you never know when it's going to be your last."

I knew she was speaking of Kai and all they had endured and nearly lost, but my thoughts wandered to Sakari. Before I could stop my mouth, I asked, "Do you regret him? Sakari, that is."

Calliope's eyes squinted as she studied me. I overstepped. "I'm sorry. It's none of my business."

"No, it's okay," she encouraged. "I just don't understand the question."

"Do you regret getting close to him?"

Calliope sighed heavily and licked her lips. "You know, I haven't really spoken about him since The Battle or dwelled too long on him. Not because I never cared, but because I cared more than I expected to." She pressed her lips tightly together, her teeth nibbling the insides. "At the risk of this coming out wrong, let me just say, I love Kai. I've always loved Kai. I was meant to be his, but if there was no Kai, I would've been lucky to have Sakari. So, to answer your question, no. I don't regret getting close to him. Sakari helped me find an inner strength I'd yet to uncover, and I miss him every day. I loved him, Sarai. Maybe I wasn't *in* love with him as he was with me, but he was one of the good ones, and I wish every day he was still here. Not for me, but for you."

"It's probably for the better." I blinked back tears and looked to the ceiling to gain my bearings. "Do not misinterpret me, Calliope. I do not say what I'm about to, to make you feel guilty, but for you to understand and feel no regret. I do not think Sakari would be happy in this life without you. He would never love another the way he loved you. I think he was grateful to have what he did with you. To be able to spend his last days with you as his wife. Not everyone in our world gets to be with the one they love or even find the one they want to spend their lives with, but Sakari did. That's all any of us could really ask for, is it not?"

"Believe me, Sarai," Calliope said in a near whisper. "Sakari deserved so much more."

SEVENTEEN

LIA

My feet had never known this kind of pain. There were blisters in places I didn't know existed. After years of living in the forest, one would think my feet had experienced it all. Apparently not. All I wanted to do was soak my feet and go to bed. Who knew serving at a restaurant could be so painful and draining? Why did I let Cameron send in an application?

Oh, right. Because it was the only job that agreed to pay me under the table.

When I opened the front door, the only light in the apartment was the glow of the TV. Cameron sat on the couch next to a girl I'd never seen before. He paused whatever was on and smiled at me, sitting forward. "Hey, how was your first day?"

I looked between the two of them. They were on my bed. I wanted to cry.

"Fine."

I found myself inspecting his date. Her long brown hair and button nose. It was dark, but I could tell she wasn't wearing a lot of make up. She was pretty. Really pretty. Not that I'd expected Cameron to date an ugly girl.

"Lia, this is Gretchen. Gretchen, Lia."

She smiled and waved, but she wasn't here to make friends. She stared back at me the same way she probably thought I was looking at her. As if I were competition. I wasn't interested in competing. I just wanted to shower and go to sleep. The child in me threw her head back and cried, stomping her foot.

This hadn't been a problem before. If any of the guys had dates, they typically took them out or went to a party or took them back to their rooms. This was the first girl Cameron brought back to the apartment who I cared about, because, for once, I needed sleep, and it was being taken away.

Cameron draped his arm along the back of the couch behind his date. Whatever he said her name was. "Lia, you can go to my room." Did I have a choice? Was he kicking me out? Or was he trying to spare me from watching him make out with his date all night? Why couldn't *he* go to his room? "You look tired," he explained. "You can sleep on my bed, and I'll come get you when Gretchen leaves."

"What are you guys watching?" Ryland came from the hall and walked into the kitchen.

"*Anonymous Alex*," Cameron answered.

"Man! You're watching it without me?" Ryland opened the fridge and grabbed a soda.

Cameron's eyes shifted from me to Ryland and then back. "You can watch it with us if you want. We just started it. You too, Lia. Unless you want to go to sleep."

Who was this nice Cameron, and what did he do with the old one? I knew we'd moved past our bitter banter, but this was still weird.

"No thanks." Number one, I *didn't* want to watch him make out with his date all night. And two, while Ryland had never hit on me like Chase, I didn't want to give him the wrong impression. The love seat was the only seating option left. I was *not* sharing it with him. "I *am* tired. Just wake me when you want to go to bed."

"Yeah, if Lia isn't watching, I'm not gonna crash your date. I've got some studying to do anyway."

"Suit yourselves."

Ryland lifted his soda in a cheers gesture and nodded at me before heading back to his room. I offered him a halfhearted smile. That was probably the most interaction we'd ever had.

I walked in front of the TV. "Let me just grab my pajamas." I felt both sets of eyes on me as I rifled through my bag by the couch. Hurrying out of the room, I offered a quick, "Night," before dashing down the hall toward the bathroom.

After sitting under the hot water for a good twenty minutes and changing into my pajama shorts and T-shirt, I closed myself in Cameron's room. I didn't even bother turning on the light before crawling into his bed. I almost forgot what a bed felt like. Heaven. It couldn't have been more than a minute after my head hit his pillow that I was out.

I hadn't slept that well in … I couldn't remember the last time I'd slept so well. I was cocooned in a cloud of softness and warmth. The couch was remarkably more comfortable than it had ever been. Breathing in deep, my body stretched out and my brain woke all the way up. Whatever was pressed to my back was not the couch I'd been sleeping on for months, but a solid, warm body. And it was curled around me, an arm slung over my waist. I jumped, elbowed his stomach, and heard a loud thud. I couldn't help my reflex. There was a curse, and I looked over the edge of the bed at Cameron lying on the floor.

"What the heck, Lia?" He peeked up at me out of one eye, wincing.

"What the heck, *Lia*? What the heck, *Cameron*! Why were you in the bed with me?"

"I'm sorry," he groaned. He sat up, propped up on one elbow and rubbed the back of his head. "You looked so comfortable, and I tried sleeping on the couch, but it sucks. And Saturday is my one day to sleep in, and I didn't want to be woken up by Chase or Ryland."

"And what do you think I've been doing for the last three months?"

Cameron leveled me with an irritated stare. "Getting free room and board."

Right. Foot in mouth. I shouldn't complain. I was grateful to have that couch. Even if I was woken up by one of the three of them or the sun that shone through blinds every morning. It was a safe, soft place to lay my head every night. *Show some gratitude, Lia.*

"Sorry. I just didn't expect to wake up in the same bed as you."

"No." He sighed, sounding apologetic. "I should've slept on the couch. And I probably would've slept longer." He looked over at the clock on his nightstand. 8:47 AM "You went to bed at like ten o'clock."

"What time did you come to bed?"

"After two."

He stood up in only a pair of sweatpants. No shirt. Had I ever seen Cameron shirtless before? If I had, I wasn't paying attention. Holy Hannah. Who knew he'd have toned muscles hiding underneath those clothes? He had a six-pack and the V. Oh gosh. Why couldn't I stop staring? He was not the first man with a bare chest I'd seen. *Stop staring, Lia!*

Gaining control of myself too late, my eyes flickered up to his after blatantly ogling, and by the smug expression on his face, he knew exactly what I'd been doing.

Please don't say something arrogant. Chase wouldn't miss the opportunity. He'd have said something egotistical and cliché like, "Enjoying the view?"

Cameron didn't take joy in my misery. He turned to his dresser and grabbed a shirt from the top drawer and put it on.

"Better?" he asked.

I scowled. Why did he have to draw attention to the elephant in the room?

"What?" He laughed. "You looked so uncomfortable. I figured you wanted me to put on a shirt. I can take it back off." His fingers gripped the hem and lifted.

"No," I stopped him. "Shirt on is better."

His licked his lips and snorted.

Flinging back the covers, I burst open Cameron's bedroom door and regretted it instantly. Chase was walking out of the bathroom across the hall with a towel around his waist.

He looked from me, standing in my wrinkled pajamas and hair that looked slept on, to Cameron in his pajamas and just woke-up-eyes, and back at me.

Perfect.

I should've walked out the door first, to make sure the coast was clear, but it hadn't crossed my mind since we had nothing to hide.

Until I saw Chase. A knowing smirk plastered across his face, except there was no knowing. Nothing had happened. So, I'd woken up before Lia with my arm across her waist and I hadn't removed it. So, what? I had been comfortable. And maybe I'd been disappointed she'd thrown me on the floor. She'd ruined a perfectly comfortable position. It didn't mean anything. And Chase needed to know that.

Lia stiffened immediately.

"No wonder you kept turning me down." He

chuckled under his breath as his eyes trailed up and down her body. I nearly punched him for that simple gesture.

"Nothing happened," I said from over her shoulder. I didn't want Chase getting the wrong idea about Lia.

"Sure, sure." Chase's grin grew wider.

Lia groaned and stormed passed him, down the hallway.

"I mean it, man. We were just talking."

Chase shrugged with an unconvinced look on his face, still smirking, and disappeared behind his bedroom door.

I cautiously approached Lia to make sure she was okay. "Forget about him, Lia. You know he's a jerk."

"I don't care," she said, clipped, as she rummaged through her bag, her shoulders tense. "I just have to be at work in an hour, and I am *not* going to be late for my second day. I'm supposed to open for the first time."

"You *do* care, or you wouldn't have stomped down the hallway like you were on your way to murder someone. I'll make sure he knows nothing happened."

"It doesn't matter. He can think whatever he wants about me. People have thought worse. Maybe if Chase thinks we're a thing, he'll stop hitting on me." She shouldered past me without looking me in the eye.

I wanted to push it, but thought better of it and let her go. I shouldn't care. Lia could take care of herself. Maybe not in all senses of the phrase—considering I got her that job, and she was still living with me for free—but when it came to holding her own against guys like Chase, she didn't need me.

Why was it, then, that I felt the need to protect her? Most likely because I could still hear Calliope's voice every time I thought about backing off. *Look out for her, Cam.* And I probably would until Lia got back on her feet and left me for good. And I wasn't about to dwell on the reason why that thought made my heart sink.

NINETEEN

SARAI

I waited for Marcus at our agreed rendezvous point so I could share with him what Calliope said about the scroll—with her permission, of course. Kayne, Galdinon, Brae, and Gallagher patrolled the perimeter to assure my safety. While I trusted my men, Marcus would be here soon with his Keepers and I'd feel much more secure with more numbers.

I was not sure why we'd thought meeting halfway was the right decision rather than in one of our own kingdoms. Marcus didn't seem to trust anyone, so he did not want any suspicion raised if he kept coming to Rymidon or if I showed up in Oraelia. It was only a matter of days before Rymidon learned of what was happening. I needed to tell them, but I didn't want to burden anyone. The security had doubled. Precautions were being taken, but I would have to inform them eventually. Families deserved to mourn their loved ones properly, if I could just get firmer answers to give them before then.

Wind whistled through limbs and leaves, giving the forest any eerily calm aura. The woodlands were a place I should feel the most at home, the most free. And yet, without being allowed in the forest all those years, it felt so foreign and unsettling.

The last time I'd spent an extended amount of time in the forest was when I was little, with Sakari and Skye. The memory was so long ago it was fuzzy. Flashes of their beaming faces clogged my mind as they vaulted off tree trunks and flipped from branches, showing off the tricks I'd yet to learn as they taunted me, watching from the ground below.

A strangled cry tore through my memory. My eyes darted to the distress call.

"Run! *Run!*"

That was all it took. I ran. As fast as my legs would carry me, with my heart beating out of my chest. I didn't know who shouted or why, and I didn't need to. Somehow I knew they didn't want to say my name, so as not to draw attention to me. I didn't know what direction I was headed, or if I was even capable of evading capture, but I ran as far as I could to get away.

Branches scratched my arms and legs as I soared past, but I didn't slow. As I pushed on, I heard them getting closer, shrubberies and twigs crunching under feet. They were close. Too close. I didn't dare glance over my shoulder to gage their distance. Instead, I picked up speed. Sakari's voice pushed me inside my head. *Run, Sarai. You are stronger than you know. Keep going. Run.*

An arm encircled my waist, and I opened my mouth to scream. Nothing came out. A hand trapped the sound. I spun into a solid body braced against a tree trunk. When my eyes trailed up, I saw Marcus place a finger over his lips to silence me as he removed his hand from my mouth. He kept his grip on my waist as he peered over his shoulder around the trunk, holding me close.

The woodlands were silent.

When he turned back to me, he didn't remove his arm from around me. He held me secure and combed the land without a word. We remained quiet for a few minutes, the tension building between us. Were they gone? What if we were found? Were my Keepers okay?

When he decided we were safe, Marcus released a heavy sigh. He didn't remove his arm around me when he quietly asked, "Did you get a look at any of the assassins?"

I shook my head. Tears began their descent down my cheeks. "One of my Keepers shouted for me to run, so that is what I did. It could have been anyone, anything."

He nodded curtly, his jaw set tight.

"What happened to my Keepers?" I asked. "Where are yours?"

"We arrived as Gallagher was being taken. My Keepers took off after them, and I ran after you."

"Gallagher." I choked on tears. "What about Kayne? Or Brae and Galdinon?"

His answer was short. "I don't know."

I buried my face in my hands. "It's as if they knew, Marcus. They knew you and I were meeting here. How is that possible?"

Marcus gently stroked the back of my head, pressing me close to his chest. "Shhh … Sarai, we cannot break down now. We need to get back to your castle. We are too vulnerable out here."

"I know. I know. I just…" Lifting my eyes to meet his, I swallowed. "I've never been faced with anything like this before. Sakari taught me how to defend myself. I'm not helpless, but it is not second nature. When you caught me, I for sure thought I was done for."

Marcus's hand held my face, his thumb hooking under my chin, and he stared intently into my eyes. "I will never let anything happen to you, Sarai. Never. You have my word."

For the first time since I lost Sakari, I felt safe. Cherished.

"My Queen."

I spun in Marcus's arms. Kayne approached, out of

breath, sweat pouring down the side of his face. "Kayne!" I threw my arms around his neck. "Oh, thank the Fallen Fae!" His arms hesitantly hugged me back.

I remembered my place and stepped away. "Where are Brae and Galdinon?"

"I hoped they were with you."

I shook my head. "Gallagher?"

Kayne's head hung. "He's gone."

"We need to go." Marcus stepped in. "My Keepers will know to meet me in Rymidon. We're not safe out in the open."

The three of us raced back to the castle. Kayne led the way, while Marcus remained behind me, ensuring my safety. When we reached the castle gates, Brae and Galdinon were outside, pacing back and forth, watching the tree line for us. Kayne embraced each of them.

"How did you make it back alive?" he asked them. "You had three of them on your trail."

Marcus pointed to the open gates. "Let's take this inside. We need to discuss what happened back there without the prying eyes of Rymidon."

I closed the doors of the gathering hall behind us and sat on my throne. "What did you see, Kayne?"

"I was headed east, in the direction of Gallagher, on my patrol when I saw the dark figures swoop in. I yelled for you to run, Your Grace, and then I darted after the captors. They were tall. Our height, if not taller. So, I think it is safe to say we can rule out the trolls. They had hooded cloaks, so I couldn't get a good look at them."

I turned to Brae and Galdinon. "What did you two see?"

"The cloaked figures came out of nowhere," Brae concurred. "I barely caught sight of them out of the corner of my eye. In one instant, Gallagher was there, the next he vanished."

"As though … he disappeared?" I asked.

He shook his head. "He didn't disappear. The attackers were simply that quick. Kayne, Galdinon, and I tried to chase after them, but they split up, and so did we to cover ground. Within a few hundred feet, they were gone without a trace."

"How many were there?" Marcus inquired.

"Three," Kayne answered. "Four, possibly. It happened too quickly."

"Did you see my Keepers in the forest? They followed the sound when they heard you shout."

They shook their heads. Brae said, "I came across Galdinon on my way back to the castle. When I only saw him, I thought we'd lost Kayne, too."

"It's possible they were able to track the attackers better than we were," Kayne said, though he didn't believe the words he said. It sounded more like he wanted to pacify Marcus. My Keepers were just as capable as

Oraelia's, if not more so, since they were once under the extreme direction of my father. He never settled for anything less than perfection when it came to protection.

Marcus set his jaw and nodded. "Hopefully, they made it back to Oraelia. Sarai, may you and I have the room?"

"Yes, of course. Will the three of you please wait outside?"

"Yes, Your Highness," they said, and backed out of the gathering hall.

"We still need to discuss why we were meeting in the first place." Marcus turned his back to the closed door. "What information did you find out from Calliope?"

"What I'm about to disclose to you cannot leave this room. Until we know how better to handle the situation. We have no idea who we can and cannot trust."

Marcus nodded, agreeing. It was the forest in his eyes. I was pulled into their depths, feeling the sincerity and honor. I could tell him anything.

"Calliope's family created a full documentation of our existence. Our history, our laws, our abilities, our heritage. It is meant only for the eyes of True Royals. She told me one of the scrolls is missing. A rather important scroll. One that documents the purpose of our blood and all its abilities, how it can be utilized. Calliope and I believe maybe whoever took the blood is trying to figure out how to wield our powers."

"Took the blood?"

Had I not mentioned the missing blood? "Was the Oraelian not drained of blood?"

"No, he was," Marcus confirmed. "But, you never mentioned yours were missing blood."

"I guess I've been holding that detail close for protective purposes."

"So, you believe the assassin drained the blood and is attempting to use it to channel our powers?" His head shook vehemently. "That's not possible."

"I thought the same thing, but why steal the scroll? Why drain the blood of every casualty if it weren't going to be used?"

The rapid rise and fall of his chest looked painful. His eyes narrowed in fear. Marcus began to pace, rubbing his neck as he wore down the wood beneath him. The anxiety pouring off him cascaded toward me. Was he formulating a solution? What did he fear? Did we have any hope? Was my information worse than he'd anticipated?

After a few minutes, I let my voice break the silence. "What are you thinking?"

His hand dragged down his face as he turned to me and sighed, like the words waiting needed more room in his lungs to form. Marcus clenched his teeth. "If they are storing the blood they've drained, and it can be transferred to any creature in any capacity, the results are endless." Dread laced his eyes. "And with the amount of blood the enemy now possesses, who knows how many creatures they could've used it on. How much blood would it require to transfer our powers?"

Where was the hint of optimism? I needed at least a fraction of reassurance that what we were dealing with would not be the end of our existence. "We need to find that scroll."

Marcus nodded. "If we're lucky, it requires a large sum of blood, but if it requires a small dose…"

"They could have transferred our blood to hundreds."

"Someone has to have noticed something out of the ordinary. Rymidon needs to be informed. It's time, Sarai. While it will cause some upset, it will raise awareness, and keep others from getting hurt. We will better be able to work together to seize the culprits."

"You're right." I nod and put on a brave face. "I will make a kingdom-wide announcement this evening."

"I can stay." Marcus paused. His expression waffled with uncertainty. Was he uncertain about staying? Or uncertain that I would want him to? "If you would like me to … to be there when you make the announcement."

I contemplated sending him back to Oraelia, so he could deliver the news as well. I could stand on my own and accept the repercussions for withholding this information from them for as long as I have. But, with Marcus's support, Rymidon would understand we were on the same side. They would see we are not the only kingdom being targeted. This was not backlash from the

Battle of Faylinn. This was an attack on us all.

One look into his eyes and I didn't want to tell him no. I wanted him with me, as a united front. And possibly a little more.

"Thank you, Marcus. I think that would be beneficial. I will have Kayne assemble everyone in the gathering hall."

He offered a smile that stirred inside of me. When he so rarely smiled, one turn of his lips felt special. As if he saved his smiles and only offered them to those who earned it. When I smiled in return, he extended his hand. It was more than a hand to hold; it was a gesture of unity. We would fight this together, as one.

TWENTY

LIA

Adrianne was giving me a rundown of my section when Cameron walked in the double doors of Amici's with his hand on the back of a new girl. I knew learning the other girl's name wasn't important. How many different girls did he have?

"Two?" Adrianne perked up, hostess mode kicking in.

"Yeah." Cameron smiled at me in a taunting way. "And can we be seated in Lia's section?"

Adrianne looked to me, either wanting an explanation or my go ahead. "This is my roommate, Cameron." And I had a feeling he was going to make me work for my tip tonight.

She looked Cameron up and down, then smiled. "Well, okay. Table or booth?"

"Booth, please," he said.

"Right this way."

I stayed at the hostess podium in case any one else came

in. Adrianne returned and stood in front of it. "You didn't mention you were rooming with Cameron Bennett."

I lifted an eyebrow, not understanding. "I hadn't realized that would mean something."

"Well." She placed her hands on either side of the podium, leaning over and whispered, "It means something to me. He's in my chem class. And he is a *looker*."

"A looker?" I laughed. "Who says that?"

Adrianne giggled. "My grandma."

"You should probably hang out with your grandma less. She's set you back a few decades."

"Whatever. My grandma is the best."

I laughed and walked to the booth where she'd sat Cameron and New Girl. "What can I get you started off to drink?"

Cameron looked like he was studying the menu very closely. His fingers stroked his chin as he pursed his lips. I knew he was going to order a Mountain Dew, so I didn't know why he bothered looking. "Hmm ... So many choices."

"I'll have a Diet Coke," New Girl said.

"What do I want, what do I want?" Cameron worked his jaw from side-to-side. Now he was just being annoying.

"I'm coming back with your date's drink, and then you can order."

"No, no ... I'll have ... hmm..."

"Cameron, I'm bringing you a Mountain Dew. I know that's what you're going to order."

He looked up from his menu. "But what if I want to try one of these Italian sodas?"

"Do you?"

Cameron grinned at me like a fool. "No."

I tried not to scowl at him, but he was making it very difficult. "If you make me work hard for this tip, I'll make you work hard for your food."

"Do I need to speak to your manager?" Amusement danced across his eyes.

"You wouldn't dare."

He chuckled. "Just bring me a Dew, please."

"You're so predictable." I turned to his date. "I'm sorry you agreed to this. He'll be obnoxious all night." And walked away.

While I was filling up their drinks behind the bar, Adam, my trainer, came up next to me. "Looks like table seven is giving you a hard time. Just remember to keep a smile on your face. It's all about customer service."

"I know him." I brushed Adam off. "We're roommates. We've been friends since high school."

For some reason, that thought struck me. So much of our time spent together was focused on what had happened in Faylinn and my deception. It was easy to forget Cameron and I had once been friends. High school felt like a lifetime ago. I mean … it was. So much had happened since then, I could hardly remember what it was like being human before. I'd had parents and a brother who thought they'd loved me. I'd lived with them for over four years, but so easily my brain had shut them out. I suppose it made sense. Adair put me in their home as a transplant. I wasn't meant to last in their lives or memories, but a piece of me missed them and the simpler life.

What would have happened if I'd never turned on Calliope? What would have happened if I'd never gone back to Rymidon? Would I still have a family?

"Whoa, whoa, Lia." A hand gripped around mine and

rested on my lower back. I shook my head, clearing my thought. The drinks had overflowed all over the soda machine. "You okay?" Adam asked and grabbed a rag close by.

"Yeah, sorry." I wiped around the glasses. "Thanks. I just spaced out for a second."

"You need me to take that table?" Adam seemed genuinely concerned. "I don't mind."

"No, I'm fine. Really. I'll take care of them."

"You sure?" Adam's hand was still on the small of my back, and suddenly it felt more intimate than friendly or concerned. "I know you're new to this stuff. Take on more tables a little at a time."

"I'm sure. I can handle it. Thanks, Adam." I ducked away. When I turned, I saw Cameron scrutinizing me. Great. He saw me spilling their drinks. More for him hold against me.

TWENTY ONE

CAMERON

After dinner, I'd dropped Emily off at her apartment. I wasn't feeling it. With as quickly as she'd jumped out of my jeep, she probably wasn't too disappointed I'd ended the night early. It was after eleven when Lia walked in the front door, and I was watching *Criminal Minds* reruns.

"Not again," she groaned.

I chuckled because the only light in the room was the TV, so she probably didn't check to see if I was alone. "I'm alone."

"Oh, thank goodness." She plopped on the couch beside me and closed her eyes, her head falling back. "I just want to wash my face and go to sleep."

"And you can do that as soon as this episode is over."

"Cameron, please. Didn't you make my night difficult enough?"

I couldn't stop my laughter. After making her describe

half the menu in detail and asking her to give us a few more minutes multiple times before she could take our order, I knew if I didn't lay off she was going to spit in my food.

"Oh, c'mon. The BAU was just about to deliver their profile on this serial killer. Wash your face and come finish it with me. Then I'll let you go to bed."

She sighed and got to her feet. She leveled me with a serious face. "Fine. Just this episode and then sleep."

"Deal."

When she came back and sat down with her knees to her chest, freshly washed of makeup, and her hair tied up on top of her head, I realized I'd never really looked at Lia without her makeup. She had a light dusting of freckles across her nose that made her look younger—innocent, even—which was comical in itself, but somehow made perfect sense. The more layers I uncovered of Lia, the more I liked.

During a commercial break, my question tumbled out without permission. "So, you get a job for a week and already have a boyfriend?"

"Huh? What are you talking about?"

I saw that server with his hands all over her when she'd been filling up our drinks behind the bar. It was no wonder she'd spilled everywhere with him practically groping her. "The brown-haired guy with the eyebrow piercing."

"Oh." Lia made a disgusted face. Good sign, good sign. "Adam?"

"Is that his name?"

"He was my trainer the first few days. He's supposed to keep tabs on me since I'm new at this whole server thing."

"Seems to me he wants to do a lot more than train you."

"No, he doesn't. Gross. And no, thank you."

I stretched my arm along the back of the couch, facing her. "You know, you can't say that about every guy forever."

She paused with her eyes glued to the screen. Why was I pressing the issue like I cared? It made sense for her to ward off guys for a while, if not forever. The love of her life just died, not that he deserved her love.

Just before the show came back on, Lia murmured, "It'll take a lot for me to trust another guy ever again."

I assumed Lia would be weary of another relationship because of her loss, but of course, she'd be weary of another manipulative jerk. Granted, Skye had been manipulative in a phenomenally horrible way when he'd convinced her to follow his dad's plan, but that didn't excuse other guys. There were lots of idiots out there. I should know. I was friends with a few of them and rooming with one of the worst womanizers I'd ever met. No one could blame Lia for being skeptical. And I hated that an unexplainable part of me wanted to be the one to change her mind.

Half an episode turned into another full episode, which turned into three more episodes.

"Wait, wait, wait," Lia said, pulling on my arm when I tried to get up after the last episode and go to bed. "But there's another one."

"And there's going to be another one after that, but I have to get up for class at nine."

"What time is it?"

"Three, and I'm already going to hate myself when I wake up."

"Dang it. How is it already three? I'm not even tired anymore." She yawned. "Okay. That was a fluke." She yawned again, and I laughed. "Shut up. Go to bed. I'm watching this without you."

"You can't do that."

"Says who?"

"The *Criminal Minds* committee. It's in the bylaws. Once a *Criminal Minds* marathon commences, the members of said marathon must only continue as one."

Lia snorted and yawned, but tried hiding it behind her hand. "Okay. Fine. But let me make it clear, I'm only stopping because I need to be mentally present at work tomorrow and sleep is taking over. Not because you asked me to."

"Whatever helps you sleep tonight." I got up from the couch and clicked off the TV.

When I got to the hallway, I turned around to say goodnight. The living room was pitch black, but I could make out the curve of Lia's figure, curling onto her side as she pulled the blanket around her and slipped a pillow beneath her head. Would it be crossing the line if I asked her to come sleep in my bed? Not in a pervy way, but I knew how uncomfortable that couch was and how hard it must be to stay asleep when the rest of us were up and about. And sleeping next to her didn't suck before.

"Why are you creepily standing in the hallway watching me?"

"Sorry." I cleared my throat. "Night, Lia."

She yawned goodnight and my name as she rolled over to face the couch. I should've turned around and walked away, but for some idiotic reason I couldn't. See. Guys were idiots.

"Do you want to sleep on my bed?"

She rolled back over. It was too dark for me to see her expression, so I couldn't tell if she was contemplating it or wanted to tell me to screw off. I could've waited for seconds, but it felt like hours of silence.

"Are you going to be sleeping in the bed, too?"

"Well … it's a queen, so it's big enough for the both of us. And it's my bed."

"Are you going to stick to your side of the bed this time?"

"We can put a pillow between us if it makes you feel any better."

Lia didn't respond. What was she thinking? I'd crossed the line, hadn't I? She was going to go off on some rant or make me feel like the idiot I was being. Any second she'd tell me how I'd made things all kinds of awkward.

"Okay," she said.

"Okay," I said back.

Neither of us moved. Was I supposed to wait for her or help her carry something? Was it more awkward if I left without another word? I turned when she started to sit up and headed for my room. I stopped and spun back to tell her to bring her pillow and collided with her.

"*Umph*," she grunted.

I reached out to grab her arms and steady us, but instead punched her in the shoulder. Hard.

"Ouch!"

"Sorry! Sorry." I rubbed the stop I'd hit. "It was an accident. I was just going to tell you to bring your pillow."

She rolled her shoulder back, away from my touch and held up the pillow, looking like she was second-guessing taking me up on my offer. "Check."

"Cool." I shouldn't have told her she could sleep in my bed. *Maybe I should take the floor. Nah.*

But, she'd agreed.

Don't let that get you excited, Cameron.

She must really hate that couch.

TWENTY TWO

SARAI

As I walked through Rymidon, checking on the families of the deceased, every home I passed was eerily quiet. Our villages weren't nearly as lively as they'd been before I'd made the announcement about the assassinations. No one was taking any risks by wandering off into the forest.

I'd hinted that they should remain cautious, but I did not want to create this much panic. If only there were enough room in that castle for everyone, so they could roam freely, without fear. Though, the assassins could be living among us. Now that everyone stayed inside, the assassins could grow bolder and attack fae in the safety of their homes. Keepers patrolled the villages in case that was to happen. It pained me to require so much security, to feel this powerless.

Having Marcus by my side when I revealed the deaths was more than comforting. It felt right to know I had his unwavering support when so many looked to me for answers. It was difficult watching him leave. Without his presence, I felt alone again. I may have Keepers on a constant rotation, but that wasn't the kind of loneliness I meant. I didn't know how to explain it to myself. The only real companionship I'd ever felt before was with Sakari, a brotherly companionship. This was different. Not deeper, or more, just … different.

Was this why it was better to have a kingdom run by two? Not to make decisions for me or take on my responsibilities, but to share the burden, to have someone on my side. A devoted, committed companion to stand by me. It was difficult to imagine doing this on my own forever. How did Calliope do it before Kai?

After the announcement, I'd asked Kayne to bring in suspicious fae I could question. We'd agreed to keep the drainage of blood a secret. It was the one piece of leverage we had to know how much others knew. So far, I had only spoken with ten possible assassins, and none of them had given me any indication they could be capable of such acts. I didn't want to believe any were capable of the assassinations, but I kept as open a mind as I could.

If no one provided any useful knowledge, or came forward soon, I would have to resort to questioning each and every Rymidonian. The thought of that made me ill. I did not want them to believe their queen distrusted them. I was supposed to bring change. To be their protector, not their accuser. And it was highly likely the assassins were not among us, so I ran the risk of falsely accusing an innocent. There was no uncomplicated answer.

"Queen Sarai, Calliope of Faylinn is here to see you."

"Kayne, she is my sister." I smiled. "You are allowed to call her Calliope, or Queen Calliope if it makes you feel more comfortable. You don't have to announce her kingdom. I know who you are speaking of."

"Yes, Your Grace." He bowed out of the room and Calliope replaced him.

We hugged. "Any closer to finding these dang ersewings?"

I slowly exhaled and pulled back. "I wish. I have spoken to ten Rymidonians and none of them gave me the feeling they were responsible. Marcus is having questionable fae in Oraelia interrogated as well."

Calliope said, "As I have asked Declan and Dugal to do, but no one in Faylinn seems to fit the crime or have any helpful info. Since the uniting celebration, it seems Faylinnians are even more open to connecting with the kingdoms. We're ready to put the past behind us and move on. In my gut, I don't feel like any of them are capable are hurting so many."

I nodded. It didn't make sense to me either, but evil never made sense to me.

"I can't help but keep coming back to the elves," Calliope said. "What if we check in with them? Sniff around a little and see if they have something to hide."

"Sniff? I do not want to sniff anywhere the elves have been."

Calliope chuckled. "Not literally. I just mean we go and investigate covertly, try not to raise suspicion that we're looking into them. See if they've had any incidents or know anything about what's happened to us. When Guthron came to me at the Awakening, it seemed the elves knew a lot more about the occurrences in our world than we did. Even if they aren't the culprits, they might lead us to our assassins."

"That is a clever proposal. Do you have Declan and Kai with you?"

"Kai is in Faylinn, holding down the fort, but Declan and Dugal came with me."

I looked at her questioningly. I doubted I would ever understand all of her human terms. "I am assuming Kai is not actually holding down a fort."

Calliope tried to hide her amusement. "No. Just taking care of royal business while I'm away."

"Okay." It made no sense, but I accepted her answer. "Someday you will have to teach me all of your human sayings, so there is no need to explain them every time."

"That may take awhile."

Calliope informed Declan of our plan to meet with Guthron when we'd invited him into the gathering hall.

"There is no *going* to see the elves," he said, sparing me a perplexed glance before giving his full attention to Calliope. "The elves find you."

"So, there's no Elves Land or some village where we can go to speak with Guthron?" Calliope asked.

"The elves don't stay in one place for long. They're too suspicious of everyone to build a village. They don't allow themselves to be caught off guard by unannounced visitors."

"So, then how do we find them?" she asked.

"We don't normally need to speak with the elves. They

are typically avoided by any means necessary. I can try to put out a call. Maybe by spreading the word that the Queen of Rymidon and the Queen of Faylinn want to speak with them, Guthron will make an appearance out of sheer curiosity."

"But, Declan, if we spread the word, everyone will want to know why. Now that we've revealed the killings, everyone will know we are suspicious of the elves. We can't risk that information leaking and someone taking matters into their own hands. The elves could be just as innocent as anyone else."

Declan heaved a sigh. "I'm not sure what you want me to say."

Calliope turned to me. "What if you position Keepers as surveillances in the places you've had killings. Not patrolling in plain sight, as usual for protection, but hidden in trees and burrows and such as prevention. Camouflaged."

"Camouflaged," I repeated, nodding. "Concealed so they cannot be snuck up on, and yet still carry out their responsibilities. I like it. I will inform Kayne to the change at once."

Declan cleared his throat.

"Yes, Declan," Calliope said.

"We already do that."

"Well, then let's increase the camouflaged fleet, or whatever and position them in the more vulnerable zones."

Declan bit back a laugh. "Yes, My Queen."

"I don't know if my Keepers already use that tactic, but they will now."

"And in the mean time, Declan," Calliope said, "maybe go through some discreet channels and tell the elves only I want to meet with them. Leave Rymidon out of it. With their history I'm not sure Guthron would be inclined to a meeting with Sarai."

He nodded his agreement. "I will do my best."

TWENTY THREE

LIA

As I was walking up the steps to the apartment, another random girl walked out the door with a dejected look on her face. It was only eight o'clock. Seemed a bit early for Cameron to kick out his date. He stood in the doorway seeing her off. His lips twitched into a smile when he saw me round the corner, and my heart tried flying out of my chest. I couldn't help it. I smiled back, but when it dawned on me he'd been on another date, I took it away.

"And victim number five-hundred and eighty-three bites the dust. I should probably go tell her she dodged a bullet."

"Are you jealous, Lee Lee?"

"What? No," I let disgust seep into my voice as I shouldered past him into the apartment. "And don't call me Lee Lee. It's obnoxious."

"I think you are, Lee Lee," he taunted and followed me

down the hall to his room. "Every time you see me with a date, or one leaving, you can't help but get fired up."

"Oh, don't flatter yourself, Bennett. I've simply noticed a pattern."

"Oh yeah? And what pattern is that?" He leaned up against the doorjamb as I gathered pajamas from my bag to change into after I showered. My hair needed to be washed desperately, as did my work clothes. They reeked of marinara sauce and onions.

"You talk about Chase being the womanizer, but I've seen you with twice as many girls as him. And he's actually had multiple dates with the same girl, while you have one, and then we'll never see her again. Talk about a track record. How many of those girls think they have a chance? Do they know once you get what you want they'll never see you again?"

"Whoa, whoa, whoa. And what exactly is it I want? Have you ever seen a girl leave my bedroom?"

I stood up to face him. "I don't have to. Why else would you date so many girls and have no repeats? You're living the college guy dream. I'm surprised you don't belong to some fraternity with that kind of turnover. They'd probably crown you Sigma Beta Kappa fraternity president!"

Cameron laughed, crossing his ankles and arms. "Wow. You're really worked up about this. Let's talk about it."

I groaned and continued digging for clean pajamas. "No, let's not." Because I didn't want to acknowledge why it got me so worked up. And I most definitely didn't want him to know why.

"Oh, c'mon, Lee Lee. This obviously upsets you, and I want to know why."

Why can't I find anything in this stupid bag! I suppressed a growl.

"How about we share and set the records straight? I'll go first. You want to know why there are so many different girls?" He paused, but didn't wait long enough for my retort. "Because after spending less than an hour with any of them, not one girl has made me want to spend more."

There was something in his tone that made me think he was trying to tell me something. What did his confession make me feel? Relief? Satisfaction? Cameron spent time with me every day. Not just because we lived together. He chose to. We'd spent hours looking through job listings when we could've done it in one. He gave me a side of his bed so I didn't have to suffer on the couch any longer. He stayed up, episode after episode, the other night even when he needed to be up for class.

Happy. I definitely felt happy.

No. *Pajamas, pajamas.* I was looking for pajamas. Cameron didn't make my heart race. He didn't make my stomach flutter. I wasn't pleased that he couldn't find someone he wanted to be with. I was reading into things. I'd essentially called him a womanizer, and he was defending himself.

"Must be a tough job spending time with so many girls. I guess you'll have to suffer through your continued search. Oh, the horror!" Why couldn't I stop yelling? "Be sure to contact Sigma Omega Pi, so they can give you some names! They've probably been through half the campus already!"

One moment I was shouting, shuffling through my duffle, the next I was pulled to my feet and Cameron was across the room, his lips pressed firmly against mine. Before I could react, he was gone, scrutinizing my expression—my paralyzed expression.

When my brain kicked back in, I demanded, "What was that for?"

"You wouldn't shut up!"

"And you thought kissing me was the answer?"

"It seemed like the best option at the time!"

"Okay!"

"Okay?" One of his eyebrows lifted.

My chest heaved with my elevated breathing. I didn't want to think about why or what it'd meant; I only wanted to do it again. I dropped my change of clothes, stepped forward, and kissed Cameron. My hands held his face to mine. He kissed me back. Our lips moved in synchronicity. His arms enveloped my waist, our bodies fusing together. I didn't want to stop kissing him.

So, I did. I put distance between us, catching my breath, and blinked up at him.

"What was that for?" Cameron uttered.

"I don't know."

"Are we going to talk about it?"

"No." I grabbed my clothes, pushed past him, across the hall into the bathroom, and slammed the door shut.

"By the way, Sigma Omega Pi isn't even a fraternity!" Cameron hollered.

I covered my ears and slid down the closed door.

What the crap just happened?

TWENTY FOUR

SARAI

Every couple of days Marcus came to Rymidon so we could share any progress and count the current deaths. It was my least and most favorite part of my week. I immensely enjoyed my time with Marcus, but our conversations held no room for levity. How could there be light when so much darkness had fallen upon us?

"You have lost six men?" I asked. My heart sunk deeper into my chest. "Callastonia has lost ten. What about Aurorali?"

"When I spoke with Cormac, he said it was eight."

"And Mirron?"

"Five, I believe."

"Do you know if Elfland has been touched? Calliope mentioned Queen Elena has strong safety measures in place for many reasons, that she once had wards around Elfland to protect them from my father. The Battle of Faylinn only intensified her desire to increase her Keepers and patrols."

Marcus hesitated before he nodded. "As far as I know, Elfland hasn't lost anyone."

"Calliope said Faylinn hasn't had any attacks either. Either it's only a matter of time, or they have targeted certain kingdoms for a reason. We lose someone every day. Our toll is up to fifteen."

So that meant … I counted up the final deaths in my head. Forty-four. We'd lost forty-four faeries, and we were no closer to discovering the assassins. Who would be next? Why couldn't we protect them?

I took a deep breath and closed my eyes. *Think, Sarai. Think like Sakari.* He would have had answers, taken control of the situation. He would have known what to do. *What am I supposed to do, Sakari?*

I felt a hand brush across my cheek. When I opened my eyes, Marcus was peering down at me, a helpless look in his eyes as he witnessed my tears.

"I apologize," I said, dabbing my eyes with my fingertips. Silly, betraying tears. *How dare they show my fragility in front of him?* "Missing Sakari is harder some days than others."

"No one is immune to loss. I understand." At his words, he turned away from me, his posture rigid and standoffish as he unhurriedly paced before me.

"Do you mean Nerida?" The question fell out before I thought to stop it, but I wanted him to know I understood. He was not alone.

Marcus's eyes cut to mine. "What do you know about Nerida?"

I opened my mouth to answer, but the blaze of anger in his eyes stopped me. "I…" Was I not supposed to know about her? Was she a secret Lia should have kept? I swallowed and began again. "I don't know much. I know she was important to you."

He steered his gaze away. The downturn of his mouth caused my fingers to twitch at my sides with need. I wanted to reverse the curve, for his grimace to disappear. If I reached out to touch his face, would he pull away?

It felt important to also tell Marcus, "And I know that she died in the Battle of Faylinn." I watched him, gaging his temperament and how receptive he would be to what I needed to say. "I need you to know how sorry I am, Marcus. There is not a day that goes by where I don't think about what my father did, where I don't wish I could have done something to stop him. I *despise* his choices every day."

Marcus's features showed no indication of whether he'd heard me as he stared blankly across the room. I watched him breathe, grieve in silence. While every part of me wanted to offer him comfort, I held back. I let him be. I was not sure if we had reached a point in our relationship where he would accept my comfort.

Minutes passed before he finally spoke. "Nerida's mother worked in the castle as a handmaiden for my mother. Her father was a Keeper in my father's guard, so Nerida grew up in the castle alongside me." His fingers laced together and unlaced, laced and unlaced again, as he slowly strode the gathering hall. Each step oozed his sorrow, smearing it across the wooden slats. "Most of the children of the castle's help stayed away from my brother, Alston, and me. They formed their own alliances and friendships, but Nerida liked to do the opposite of what was normal or expected of her. Rather than sitting with her mother, a weaver, and learning how to stitch clothing, or sitting in to learn the ways of a handmaiden, Nerida wanted me teach her how to spar, how to shoot a bow and arrow, how to wield a sword. They were all things I was learning at the time, so it was stimulating to have my own apprentice. As a result, we became inseparable."

Marcus offered a strained smile that halted before touching his eyes. "As we grew older and began to form a deeper connection, the reality that we'd never be able to be together grew. While Oraelia is open to bonds between other colonies, as a Royal—"

I knowingly nodded. "You must bond with another Royal to keep peace among the other kingdoms."

He nodded once, his eyes cutting to the ground. "For a long time we hid our relationship from everyone. At first, it was exhilarating to have the secrecy. In a world where every move I made was monitored, Nerida and I found our forbidden love to be the one thing we could call our own. We fiercely guarded it."

It was difficult to tell if my heart was breaking because I knew the end of their story or if my heart was grasping the truth. I may never know that kind of love. Marcus's heart was given away long ago.

I heard his throat clear. "Once I became the proper age of bonding, and I comprehended the depth of my love for her, I knew we had to end it. I had a duty to my kingdom. I'd known the duty my whole life. We fought all the time about it. Even if my parents accepted our bond, it could never be. The law prohibited it. It eventually became necessary to sever ties. I accepted the fact that it was time to move forward, and I pushed her to do the same."

"Some time later she was bound to a Craftsmen named

Kheelan and bore a child. It was around the time Calliope inherited the throne of Faylinn. When we wound up in Faylinn after the Waking Oak was poisoned and the war broke out, Kheelan and I begged Nerida to hide out with their newborn son. In true Nerida form, she refused. She sent her son, Doyle, away with her mother and fought beside us until the end."

Unable to force my voice to work properly, I whispered, "What happened to Kheelan?"

His jaw clenched, more in pain than anger. "He survived, but he blames me for not doing a better job of protecting Nerida."

"He cannot put that on you." I found my voice. "That is undeserved. I am sure you did what you could."

Marcus sighed, tormented between agreeing with me and accepting the responsibility. "Kheelan and I joined forces to shield Nerida the best we could during the battle, but he's a craftsmen, not a trained warrior. He was no match for the war in Faylinn. So, I spent my time not only protecting Nerida, but also trying to protect Kheelan. Doyle wasn't going to lose either parent on my watch." His bottom lip quivered, so he bit it and swallowed. "But … the battleground was pure chaos if you recall."

"I wasn't there." My confession made me feel guilty. I should've have been there, fighting for the right side against my father. To the outsider I must appear so sheltered.

"Well, it took everything just to keep myself alive. I turned my back on Nerida for seconds, it seemed." He paused, staring vacantly over my shoulder. "Seconds." Tears strained his ragged whisper.

Marcus didn't finish. Whether because he couldn't say the words or he knew I understood well enough. The agony in his eyes urged my arms around him. He didn't reciprocate the contact, but that did not deter me. I wasn't sure if I was hugging him to diminish his pain or mine, begging him for forgiveness. Maybe indirectly, but his loss fell on me. My father. My kingdom.

We were the reason Nerida was gone.

His arms gradually wrapped around me, his hold as fierce as mine.

"I am so deeply sorry, Marcus," I murmured, my voice raspy with remorse. "So *deeply* sorry."

His head shook, but he stayed in place, wrapped in my arms. My head moved with the irregular rise and fall of his breathing.

"I wish I had paid more attention," I whispered into his chest. "I wish I could have seen signs or known what to look for. I could have done more to prevent every loss."

Marcus pulled back and looked sternly at me; his head shook vehemently. "The Battle of Faylinn was not your fault, Sarai. After spending much time with you, that is one truth I've grown to learn. It was the result of a nefarious king who abused his Supremacy. There is nothing you could have done. Simply because you were related does not mean the blame is yours to carry. You must stop taking on the sins of your father."

"It is very difficult to do when every day I see the faces of everyone who was affected, who was hurt by the hand of my family. They stare at me like they are waiting for me to fail them." I couldn't keep my voice firm. It shook with my tears.

Marcus tilted his head down to make us eye level. His strong finger hooked under my chin so I had no choice but to look him in the eyes. Stern, but gentle enough, Marcus said,

"The expression on the faces you see is not expectation of failure; it's hope, Sarai. Over the last few weeks, I've witnessed a queen unlike any other. You are the glimmer of hope Rymidon needs. Fight for you. Fight for your kingdom," he said fervently. "Stop dwelling on the past and the iniquities of others. None of that is important. The future you choose to build is."

His mouth was there, so I pressed mine to it without thought. His perfect mouth. It tasted like faith and conviction. Two things I'd craved more than anything since I had taken my place as queen. Then my brain caught up with my body, and I retreated.

"I am sorry." Eyes wide, I covered my lips with my fingertips. "I am not sure what came over me. It was inappropriate of me to be so forward."

One breath passed his lips. Marcus grabbed the back of my neck and forced his mouth onto mine. The most passionate, and yet tender force. I inhaled, and his tongue swooped in, devouring me. My hands latched onto his biceps to remain standing while my legs wanted to give way. His lips were warm and demanding and entirely irresistible. I couldn't breathe until he released me and ran his nose unhurriedly along the length of my nose before pressing his forehead against mine.

"I want you to know my heart let go of Nerida long ago. My heart is free to love anyone it chooses. Within the Royal circles, of course." The corner of his mouth turned up at his joke. Which was sadly true.

I smiled back, a blush filling my cheeks. "Of course."

I thought of how the counsel made an exception for Calliope and Kai. Had Marcus tried, would they have made an exception for him and Nerida? Granted, Calliope had extenuating circumstances, but surely King Ronan and Queen Aislinn would have attempted to build a justification for them. Queen Aislinn knew better than any about bonding for love. It was how Oraelia came to be during The Great Divide, so she could be with King Ronan. Selfishly, I didn't want to think about that possibility. If Marcus had fought to be with Nerida, then he would not be a possibility for me.

Marcus's mouth covered mine again as he looped his arm around my waist. I welcomed the soft curvature of his lips and the skill they possessed as he placed his claim on me. His hand traced the edge of my wings, sending a shiver down my spine. A groan of desire escaped me and my fingers dug into his back.

I had never been kissed by another, so there was no one for me to compare Marcus to, but I could not imagine anyone capable of surpassing this feeling.

With a soft brush of his lips, Marcus loosened his hold and stepped back. He heavily exhaled. "Forgive me, Sarai," he whispered and let go. When I opened my eyes, I saw his retreating figure as he strode out of the gathering hall.

Had I misunderstood? What had I done wrong?

He was gone before I could muster a goodbye.

TWENTY FIVE

LIA

After work, a stump called my name to sit, so I pulled out my ribbon, feeling the softness between my fingers, and breathed in the woodlands.

I couldn't believe I'd kissed Cameron last night. Technically, he'd kissed me first, but that had been to shut me up. It could've gotten him slapped, and yet he'd done it anyway. But, I'd kissed him because I hadn't been able to stop myself. I'd had to do it. I'd wanted to do it. And I'd liked it. What had I been thinking?

I lived with the guy. Most of the time he couldn't stand me. He was helping me get back on my feet because Calliope forced him to. How was I going to walk back into the apartment and pretend nothing had happened? I couldn't. There was no way Cameron would let it go. He would find some way to mess with me. He loved pushing my buttons too much. I'd never hear the end of it. I had to move out. It was time. I'd find an apartment—maybe find a roommate to split the rent. I'd have to wait for my first paycheck, but I could make it happen. As soon as I got back to the apartment, I'd start the apartment hunt. Cameron would probably lead the search like he'd done with my job. He couldn't wait to get rid of me.

An ache grew in my chest the more I thought about moving out and the thought of it making Cameron happy. I didn't want him to be happy I was leaving. How could I want to stay?

If he hadn't left after I'd gone into the bathroom to shower, I wouldn't have been able to face him. Thankfully, I had peacefully *pretended* to be asleep on my side of the bed, pillows tucked behind my back when he'd come to sleep. The mattress had jostled, and he'd whispered my name, but I'd breathed heavier to prove I was, in fact, asleep. And I'd slipped out before he woke up in the morning. Just another hour and I'd have the courage to go home and tell him I was leaving.

There was rustling in the trees. Not the wind. Not a tiny animal. Then there was a crunch. I could decipher every sound of the forest and that was not one of natural causes. I got to my feet, alert.

"Who's there?" The rustling stopped. "Calliope?" I hoped, but my gut knew it wasn't. I was met with more silence. "Show yourself."

Four figures appeared around a tree, two flanking each side. It wasn't the familiar figures I'd expected to see.

I reared back. "What are you doing here?"

"We have a proposition for you, Lia."

"How do you know who I am?"

"We know a lot about you. And we have something we think you might be interested in."

I discreetly looked for a sharp stick or a rock heavy enough to protect myself. "How could you have anything I'd want?"

The tallest one stepped forward, remaining at the edge of the tree line. "We have a cure, a way for you to transform. You could become a faery once again, the way you were always intended."

What? "How? I've already used my changes. I'm stuck as a human."

His lip curled up in what I think he believed was a smile, but looked more sinister. "That's what you've been led to believe, but we have the cure. We can help you change back. For good."

My heart pushed against my ribcage, asking for freedom. Begging to live in the body it'd originated in. "But how? That's impossible. If it were true, I'd already be a faery."

"You'd have to trust us. The right amount and you'll never have to be human again."

I hesitated. It was too good to be true. There was no other power than the pastelline lily and Lake Haven that could change us. Everyone knew that. And if there was, why did *they* have the cure?

"You want to return to Rymidon, don't you?" he attempted to entice me, noting my reluctance.

And it worked. *I do, don't I?* I've been surviving here, but I was a fish out of water. I could only pretend for so long. I didn't belong here. Fake it until you make it, wasn't working for me.

There had to be a catch. I couldn't fall for another

corrupt deal. I'd learned my lesson. No one else would suffer because of me. If it sounded too good to be true, it most likely was. "Why are you coming to me? What's in it for you?"

"The joy of returning a faery to her true self."

"That's it?" I scoffed. "Yeah, right."

"It's true. We know what you did, why you've become a human every time. We know neither times were because you wanted this life, a human life. It always came at a price. First, as a contract to bond with your true love. Then, the second time, to gain forgiveness, redemption for your iniquities. You don't truly want this life, and we want to rectify that. Being fae is who you are. The forest calls to you."

I didn't experience the same sort of pull to the forest now as I did when I was a faery, but the distant longing still pumped through my veins. Why else would I continue to seek solace at the tree line? Being fae would always be a part of who I was.

"We have one thing we will ask of you," he added.

I shook my head and snorted my laughter. The catch. "Of course you do."

"We'd like you to help us gain favor with Queen Sarai."

I scoffed. "You realize I'm not exactly on great terms with Sarai, right? I was in love with her wicked brother, who killed her beloved brother, and helped him carry out her father's evil plan. If I'm your only option, you're kind of screwed."

"I think you have more sway than you realize."

What were they talking about? I had no *sway* with Sarai. We'd had one conversation since Skye died. Our relationship was superficial at best.

My lips pinched together. "I'll do my best, but how do I know I can trust you? How do I know this cure won't change me into something unspeakable?"

"We can show you. If you come with us, we have someone who is ready to make the change. We'll allow you to watch the transformation and make the decision for yourself. We have nothing to hide."

What did I have to lose?

One unexpected answer crossed my mind.

Cameron.

TWENTY SIX

CAMERON

Lia never came home after work. One kiss and she'd disappeared. Who would've thought Lia scared so easily? But a nagging thought wouldn't let me go. It was four hours past the time she normally took to get home. She hadn't mentioned that she was going anywhere after work. Though, she'd gone before I'd gotten up this morning, which was unusual in itself. But, she could've had somewhere to be. I still felt unsettled.

Since she didn't have a cell phone yet, I decided to show up at the restaurant. Maybe she'd picked up another shift to avoid me. It would've been so like her to dodge me after our kiss. I didn't know what to make of it either. It was why I left last night. I had to figure out what I was feeling and the real reason I'd kissed her and I'd cared enough to talk about it now. To see what it meant to her, if anything. Because I knew it'd meant a whole lot to me.

When I walked into Amici's, Lia wasn't there. Adrianne stood behind the hostess podium and told me she'd left hours ago. It wasn't like she checked in with me regularly, so I shouldn't worry. I still did.

Where could she have gone?

Maybe she'd gone back to the apartment, and we'd missed each other in passing. But, when I opened the door of the apartment and called out her name, there was no response. When I checked my bedroom, my bed was still unmade, the way I'd left it this morning. Her clothes stayed tucked away in her duffle bag on my floor, untouched.

For all I knew, she'd gone grocery shopping or had a hot date. Ha. Not likely. Maybe she'd decided to visit the forest. When she needed time to think, that was where she went, right? She couldn't avoid me forever. I wanted to talk about that kiss.

She'd kissed me back.

And then had initiated another kiss.

Why had she stopped?

As I trekked across the grass toward the set of old oak trees she always sat in front of, I searched up and down the woods for any sign of her. There wasn't a soul. Lia wouldn't have gone into the forest alone, though, right? She knew better than anyone what she could find, or rather, who could find *her*. And without the same abilities she'd once had, Lia couldn't protect herself the same way. Would she have done it anyway to sate her need to be closer to the trees? Probably.

I took one step over the tree line. "Lia?" The wind rustled the leaves. "Lia?" I cupped my hand over my mouth, calling out louder.

Nothing.

My heart started to do this erratic beating thing, and my hands started to fidget at my sides. What if something had happened to her?

"Lia!" I closed my eyes, shutting down all other senses, hoping to hear something. "Lia!" Anything. "Lia!"

Nothing.

My heart slumped when another thought crossed my mind. What if she'd finally moved away? We hadn't talked about her moving over the last couple weeks, but that didn't mean anything. Lia never told me anything. I knew it was always inevitable. She didn't want to be dependent on me forever. She was finally capable of surviving on her own. This was her opportunity to take it. I needed to accept she wasn't always going to be around.

I turned away from the green to head back to my apartment. All I could do was wait. Not patiently, because that wasn't in my nature, but she could show up soon. If she decided to leave, she wouldn't have left without all of her stuff. She couldn't have wanted to avoid me that badly. *Yeah, she might have.*

Watching my step around a fallen tree, a reddish-orange strand of material flapping in the wind caught my eye. I reached down to pick up the familiar ribbon snagged on a bush. Lia's ribbon.

Panic surged through me. I spun around. "Lia!"

129

TWENTY SEVEN

SARAI

"Prince Marcus is here to see you, Your Majesty."

At the mention of his name, my body filled with heat and anticipation. I cleared my throat to refrain from sounding affected by Marcus's expected presence. "Send him in, Kayne."

Marcus's broad figure filled the doorway, a glow from the corridor illuminating around him. Kayne closed the door when Marcus stepped inside, giving us privacy.

"Marcus," I walked toward him, "it is good to see you so unexpectedly."

"Sarai." My name was a ragged whisper. Looking closer, the whites of his eyes were red with dark rims below them. His normal kept and formal countenance was absent.

Oh, no. What happened? Who died? Another assassination? Was he hurt?

All of these thoughts flew through my mind, but I didn't

get to question him. In two steps Marcus had me in his arms, and his lips covered mine, vaporizing every thought. Gasping, I curled my hands around his arms. Marcus kissed me like I could disappear with my thoughts. Every nip and taste and stroke was more urgent than the last. His fingers gripped the back of my dress so tightly I heard stitches pop. Our bodies molded into one. If not for his hold on me, I would've been a puddle on the floor. I couldn't keep up with his urgency, so I let his mouth take control. I was at his mercy.

Over too soon, he broke away, breathing heavily. "Forgive me." His panting fell across my swollen lips.

I pecked him once to offer him confirmation. I would not bestow any forgiveness. He had no reason to be sorry, unless he was apologizing for leaving so unexpectedly days prior.

"I believe that makes us even," I said, my mind revisiting our last kiss and my presumptuousness. Not to mention his sudden departure.

Marcus laughed. At least I thought that was what it was. It sounded strange, self-deprecating. "Sarai." My name was a plea.

"Marcus?" I questioned.

"You are so beautiful." His words touched my wet lips. They were only words, and yet, they reached inside my body and stirred around the butterflies lying in wait.

"That kiss was perhaps poor timing, but I want you to know I do not mourn Nerida as the love of my life. I mourn her as my best friend." He kissed the side of my head.

I shook my head. "You already told me. You do not owe me any explanations, Marcus. I kissed you first. *My* timing was poor."

"You did not do anything I haven't wanted to do for a

long time. I kissed you today because it pained me to refrain for another second, and I knew it might be my last. I shouldn't have, and I fear as soon as I tell you why I kissed you, you will never forgive me, Sarai." Why did my name continually sound so painful for him to say?

"That is unlikely." I smiled to reassure him, even though his words weighed on me. He could tell me anything. I wanted this. Maybe our timing was poor since we were in the middle of a search for faery assassins, but I was going to listen to Calliope and take the opportunity before I lost it.

Marcus did not smile back. His arms dropped from around me as he stepped away. I did not like this maneuver. I wanted him pressed against me. Before I could take a step closer to him, he said, "I know who is behind the assassinations. I've known all along."

"I don't … I don't understand." I shook my head. If I shook it hard enough, would his words make sense? Could I un-hear his confession?

"I was vastly bitter after the Battle of Faylinn. Rymidon losing the war wasn't enough for me. I would've done anything to avenge Nerida's death."

What was he saying? There wasn't enough oxygen in my lungs to pump to my brain. No ability for me to form complete thoughts.

"When Guthron approached me, I thought they were only going to target Adair's men. He said they knew the difference between the ones who truly followed Adair and those who were under his Supremacy. I didn't know you, Sarai. I didn't know enough about Rymidon. I thought I was justified."

Justified? I couldn't see Marcus. A layer of tears obscured

my vision. No matter how many times I blinked, more tears emerged. My head wouldn't stop shaking. I couldn't believe the words coming out of his mouth.

"They needed someone inside Rymidon to steer away suspicion, to buy them time while they took out his men one-by-one. I didn't know they were taking our blood. As soon as you told me the blood of the faeries was drained, I realized I was on the wrong side. I confronted Guthron, but he refused to tell me why. I held no grounds to force him or any of the other elves. They could've exposed me or disposed of me. Sarai, if I had known their plan, you have to know I never would have stood behind them."

Words lodged in my throat. Inside, I was screaming, but I couldn't force my mouth to move.

"Please say something, Sarai. Please."

I didn't bother to wipe my eyes. "The other kingdoms? The other deaths?"

He shook head and nervously licked his lips. "I lied. None of the other kingdoms were targeted. Only Rymidon."

"Not even Oraelia?" I rasped.

He answered with another shake, his head lowering.

"And now? Why are you disclosing this to me now?" I demanded. I couldn't control the volume of my voice. My throat no longer understood the meaning of calm. "Do you expect my forgiveness? Because you will never get that from me. You betrayed *me*, Marcus. I am *not* my father. You said so yourself. And yet you stood before me over and over again pretending to help, pretending to be ignorant, watching my distress and sorrow. I trusted you. Fully!"

"I know. I know. I don't expect your forgiveness. I could beg for it, but I know I don't deserve it. I'd never ask that of you."

I clenched my teeth, willing myself to stop crying. "How gullible you must think I am, taking everything you said at face value." Why did I not have Kayne continue contacting the other kingdoms? "What kind of queen is so easily taken advantage of?"

"No, Sarai. Do not do that. I gave you every reason to trust me. And as hard as it will be now, I need you to try to trust me again. I came to tell you all of this because the elves have found the right amount of blood needed to change."

"They have the scroll? All of the elves are changing?" I choked.

"As well as some faeries who were changed to humans and no longer had the ability to change back. Guthron finally trusted me enough to disclose their purpose."

"Why?" I spat. "What is the purpose?"

"Guthron wants to create an army. They are coming to destroy Rymidon. They are tired of being the inferior race, of being deprived of their own kingdom. Once they conquer Rymidon, I fear they will move onto the next kingdom. But if we can stop them before they begin changing, they won't have an army. We can seize the blood and secure it in a safe place and destroy the scroll."

"But they already have the knowledge needed. What is to keep them from continuing their crusade? We cannot take them all out, Marcus. I do not want another war!"

"Maybe it won't come to that," he said, contemplative.

I turned from him. I couldn't look at him any longer. Looking at Marcus hurt. "How do I know I can even trust you now? How do I know the elves did not send you in here to … I don't know! Throw us off? Lure us into a trap?"

"Why would I disgrace my honor beforehand by admitting what I did? Why confess at all if my plan was succeeding. I have no desire to hurt you, Sarai. Let me make this right."

"You already hurt me, Marcus. You betrayed me! You put my entire kingdom in danger. How will I know if the Rymidonians who were killed were Adair sympathizers? For all you know, the elves lied to you. And even if they were supporters of my father, it does *not* give you the right to have them put to death! The war caused enough bloodshed. As their queen, that should have been *my* decision. Not yours!"

All he could do was nod. He looked so pathetic, and I could not revel in his misery. I was too livid with him to care.

"You're right. And I'll never forgive myself. I let the wrong emotions consume me. I should have come directly to you, but the deal was made hastily, and before I knew you existed. And when we first met I couldn't trust you. For all I knew, you were just like your father."

"You should have tried. And now we have to deal with the elves, and I don't know if I can put my faith in you again to help me do that."

"I know it's difficult, Sarai. You have every reason to turn your back on me, but because of me, every kingdom is now in danger. *I* have to fix this. It's my responsibility to make it right. I do not want anyone else harmed. I swear on Oraelia, I can keep us from entering into another war."

With each deep breath I tried to draw in, my chest constricted. Shooting pains spread through my heart. "Your plan better work, otherwise I am holding you accountable. Everyone will know what you did."

"I will not let you down. I promise."

His promise meant nothing. And my threat was empty. No one could ever know what Marcus had done. None of the kingdoms could ever know the power of our blood and what could happen should it fall into the wrong hands.

TWENTY EIGHT

CAMERON

"C'mon." I tapped my foot. "C'mon, c'mon, c'mon. Where are you, Callie?"

What was taking her so long? Did Dugal drag his feet all the way through Faylinn? I'd told him he needed to fly like the wind. My legs couldn't handle standing still. I paced back and forth, scouring the woods for any sight of her.

I flashed the light on my cellphone. It'd been an hour. She should've been here by now. Couldn't she appear out of thin air now with that door in her castle?

"What is it, Cameron? What's wrong?"

Spinning around, I saw Calliope flip down from a tree limb. "Took you long enough! It's Lia. I think she's been kidnapped."

"Kidnapped?" Calliope drew back, confused. "By who?"

"I don't know! She left for work this morning. And she

was supposed to be home *five* hours ago. First, I went to her work. They said she'd left hours before. I went back home and all of her stuff is still at my apartment. So, then I went to the trees where she always sits. It calms her down," I explained. "She wasn't there, but when I wandered into the forest I found this." I pulled out Lia's ribbon. Calliope looked at me like I was crazy. "It's Lia's. She says it reminds her of her wings. She carries it with her everywhere she goes. She wouldn't have left it behind."

"And so you think because you found this ribbon in the forest, someone kidnapped Lia? Who would do that?"

"I don't know, Cal! Just do something about it. Ask your people. Someone has to have her, someone has to know."

"I'm listening to you, Cam, but there's no reason for someone to take her."

"No reason? Doesn't everyone blame her for spying on you and essentially being the catalyst for the war?"

"Well, some, yes, but there are serious consequences. No one is allowed to touch Lia. She's suffered enough. We all have."

"That doesn't mean they wouldn't try. Callie, I know I sound crazy. I know this doesn't make sense, but I know Lia well enough now to know she wouldn't leave without saying goodbye. She *just* got a job. She was finally putting down some roots. She wouldn't leave behind all of her stuff unless she was forced to go."

Calliope finally grasped my desperation. "Okay, okay." She held out her hands to calm me down. "I'll see what I can find out."

"Let me come with you."

"Shouldn't you stay in case she comes back?"

"Please let me come, Cal. At least for a day or so. With you, I can be proactive. If I stay at home, all I'll do is worry. There's nowhere else for me to look for her. She doesn't have a car. She walks to work. I can't file a police report, not that it would do any good, considering I don't have any pictures of her, and there would be no record of her anywhere."

"Cam, there are a lot of dangerous things going on in the faery world right now. I don't feel safe bringing you into it."

"What kind of dangerous things?"

Calliope sighed. "There have been a lot of sporadic killings. Faeries left with their throats slashed, drained of blood."

"All the more reason why finding Lia is so important. What if someone is after her? What if this is trickling down from the war?"

"Cam, it's not. All the kingdoms are being targeted, not just Rymidon."

"Even Faylinn?"

"Well, we haven't had any killings yet, but it's only a matter of time. Sarai's kingdom has already lost fifteen."

"Cal, you have to have some sort of connection here. I don't know how, but Lia got tangled up in it. For all we know she could be the next Rymidonite—"

"Rymidonian," she corrected.

"Whatever. She could be the next one to wind up dead. You *have* to take me with you. I know in my gut she's not here. She's there. I was supposed to take care of her for you, and I didn't. I can't just sit here on my butt and do nothing."

Calliope heaved a sigh. "Fine. Let's go."

TWENTY NINE

SARAI

I did not wait for proper introductions. I burst past Calliope's Keepers and into the atrium.

Calliope jumped up from her desk at my sudden entrance. "Sarai, what are you doing here?"

"We need to talk," I said, my sight catching others in the room. Kai reclining on the couch, Declan standing by Calliope's side, and Cameron sitting on the window seat. "What is Cameron doing here?"

Calliope pressed her fingers into the side of her temple, looking exhausted. "Lia's missing. He thinks someone here kidnapped her."

Oh, no. Oh, no. No, no, no. "Calliope, I need to speak with you *alone*. Now."

Understanding lit her eyes. She turned her focus to Cameron. "Just wait outside, Cameron. I'll come get you in a minute."

"No, I'm not stupid." He planted himself on the seat, his arms folded across his chest, his feet flat on the floor. "If this is about Lia, I want to know. Don't keep me in the dark. *Please.*" One of Calliope's Keepers would be forced to pick him up and drag him out of here, and we didn't have any more time to lose. We would have to tell Cameron eventually.

"Okay," I relented, not wanting to fight. "But your Keepers need to wait outside."

Calliope nodded to Declan, and he backed out of the atrium with the rest of the Keepers.

"If he's staying, I'm staying," Kai asserted, walking across the atrium and sidling next to Cameron with his arms folded.

"I assumed as much." I waited until the door closed and took a deep breath. "Marcus lied to me. Rymidon is the only kingdom being targeted. He hasn't been in contact with any of the other kingdoms. Not even Oraelia has lost anyone."

"Wait a minute. What are you talking about?" Calliope asked. "Why would Marcus lie to you about that?"

While tears wanted to fall, I held them back, letting my anger squash their release. "He has been on their side the whole time. Marcus has been working with the enemy: the elves. They are planning to create an army by using our blood to change them, as well as adding faeries—who changed to humans and couldn't change back—to aid their cause. I don't believe the faeries know what they are getting themselves into."

Calliope wasn't grasping the truth. Her head shook, and her brow pinched. "Why would Marcus do something like this? It doesn't make any sense."

"Marcus wanted every last one of my father's followers,

the ones who didn't need to be under his Supremacy, to pay for the people he lost. The *person* he lost."

"Nerida," Calliope breathed.

I nodded. "Somehow Guthron knew to recruit Marcus after the Battle. His disdain for Rymidon must have been very vocal."

"So, why did he tell you this now?"

It was difficult not to shake with rage as I spoke. I wanted everything Marcus had confessed to vanish, to be a nightmare my mind had conjured up. I wanted what he'd said to be a lie.

"Marcus claims he didn't know Guthron was creating an army, or that they were going to take our blood. Apparently Marcus was put in place as an 'ally' to throw us off. And Marcus had no qualms with betraying his own kind if it meant revenge for Nerida."

"You don't believe that Marcus was unaware of their agenda?"

"I cannot trust anything that comes out of his mouth. He betrayed me, Calliope!"

My outburst stunned her into silence.

"I am sorry. It has been a very stressful day. He left Rymidon, and I came straight here."

"But, why?" Kai demanded. "Why do the elves want to begin a war? What have we done to them?"

"The elves are tired of being the 'inferior' race. They want our powers. Marcus says they've been experimenting since the Battle of Faylinn and have finally discovered the correct amount of blood to use so they can change. He wanted to warn me so we can stop them before the full army is created." I scoffed. Some timing he had. "He knows they will begin with attacking Rymidon, but he doesn't believe they'll stop there.

Marcus thinks they will move down the line. One kingdom to the next, until the elves rule our domain."

"So, you think they have Lia?" Cameron asked.

"It is very possible, Cameron. If they approached her, would she be willing to take the risk to be fae again?"

"I can't imagine Lia leaving with the elves, especially considering Rymidon and the elves haven't been on the best terms for quite some time," Calliope said. "Not to mention, they're terrifying."

"I don't know how they've swayed our kind to change and fight with them, unless it's some blood oath. *We gave you back this life, now you owe us.* Lia may have been desperate enough to have this life back. All I know is Marcus is concerned, and that concerns me."

Calliope paled. "We can't let our kingdoms know the elves have the power to transform. Who knows who else would be able to use the scroll against us?"

"I don't know how to stop that from happening."

"What did Marcus say?"

"That he would be our inside man. He told me where the elves are. He doesn't know where the blood is being stored, but he knows where Guthron is hiding. For all I know, he is still lying to me and this is a trap."

"You don't trust him at all?" Calliope asked.

"Could you? All of this time he has been strategizing with me and lending support, and it was all a lie. Everything he's done for me has been for his own gain."

"Okay," Kai said with confidence. "Then here's what we're going to do."

As Kai laid out his plan, I could hear Sakari in his voice. As if Sakari had possessed Kai's soul to come and lend his comfort and assertiveness, to let me know I wasn't forgotten. I wasn't alone.

THIRTY

LIA

I was beginning to wonder if I had a death wish or if I was just plain stupid.

This cure could either not work at all or kill me, and here I was traipsing into Rymidon's sworn enemy's lair with no form of protection, like it was another day exploring the forest. *Smart, Lia. Really smart.*

"Are you having second thoughts?" Spiky Ears asked when I slowed my pace.

I didn't care enough to know names, but I was going to have to come up with better nicknames if I was going to differentiate one from the other. Though, that seemed a little pointless considering they all looked the same to me, and I could be dead in ten minutes.

"Questioning my sanity, but not second-guessing."

"I'm sure Guthron will ease your mind."

Doubtful. Something told me meeting the king of the elves wasn't going to make me feel any better. If Cameron knew what I was doing, I'd never hear the end of how reckless I was being. But, the possibility of having my life back was worth the risk of death. If it worked for whoever they were going to change, there was nothing to hold me back.

Yes, there is.

I quieted my thoughts. This was what I wanted, no matter who I left behind. This was the life I needed, the life I craved.

The elves led me to the mouth of a wide cave. "Follow us."

Not sure what else I was supposed to do.

Walking through the opening, the inside of the stone hill expanded. Torches lined the inside, marking our path. The farther we walked, the larger the tunnel was until it opened into a gigantic room full of elves. One elf stuck out from the rest. He wielded power as he stood in front of the silent gathering welcoming me. All eyes were on me.

He extended his hand, but I didn't take it. His fingers were long with sharp nails. For all I knew he would stab me with them. "I am Guthron. It is a pleasure to meet you, Lia."

It wasn't a pleasure to meet the king of the elves, so I only nodded. He dropped his hand.

"Tarron is about to make the transformation. I understand you would like to watch before making the transformation yourself."

I nodded wordlessly.

Guthron gestured for one of the spiky ears to step forward. He was holding a large syringe filled with a thick, dark liquid and approached a human standing off to the side of the gathering. Tarron stood skeptically before he looked to

Guthron for instruction.

"Malachi, this time use every last drop. Do not let a single drop go to waste." His tone was more of a warning. What would happen if he didn't inject it all?

"What is Malachi going to do with the syringe?" I asked, hushed.

"He's going to inject into Tarron's heart."

"He's going to stick that thing into his heart?"

"Seems as though it should be more complicated?"

"No." My head shook. "It seems it should be less evasive. There was pain before, but all I've needed to do was take the pastelline lily to Lake Haven and immerse myself. Now you're saying Malachi is going to stick a giant needle into my heart."

"I didn't say there wouldn't be pain or consequences. Every transformation has been different so far. There is the risk that you will not survive."

Of course. "It would've been nice had your men mentioned that detail when they came to find me."

"Would it have changed your mind?"

A giant needle to my heart? Death or my life back? I'd already decided. It was worth the risk. At least now I knew death was most definitely a possibility. I shook my head in response.

Malachi looked to Guthron for the go-ahead. Guthron nodded, and Malachi thrust the syringe into Tarron's chest. He cried out. One second he was upright, the next he fell to the ground. I lunged for him on instinct, but Guthron held my arm back.

"My men will take care of him." Several elves rounded Tarron, picking up his legs and arms and laying him on a slab of rock in the corner. Malachi was given another syringe, and he injected the second one, careful to utilize the entire cure.

"The transformation will begin soon," Guthron said to me.

It didn't take long. His eyes remained closed, but his body jerked like he was having a seizure. Tarron thrashed from side to side. No one looked concerned or made a move to help him. They were expecting this. How many times had this taken place?

Soon, points began to develop on the tops of his ears and the color of his skin deepened, turning his pale skin tanner. His body eventually stopped convulsing, and he remained still. Was he dead?

"It'll take awhile for him to wake. His body needs time to rest and fully accept the change. We can proceed with you now or wait if you'd like."

I'd seen enough. The human was now a faery. I couldn't wait any longer. "It's all right. I'm ready."

Another one of the other spiky ears brought Guthron a new syringe. This felt very *Little Mermaid*-ish. Guthron holding my new life in his hands like Ursula gave Ariel legs. All I needed to do was sign on the dotted line, give him my voice, and I could be fae again. In a manner of speaking.

"Can I see it?"

Guthron held it out for me. My fingers inspected the large glass tube. "It's warm."

"It needs to be fresh fae blood."

Fresh *faery* blood? I stopped, my hand pulling back from the syringe. "They didn't tell me it was faery blood."

Guthron smiled. At least, I thought that's what it was. His fang-like teeth made it difficult to decipher between a smile and a sneer. "How else would you be able to transform back to fae? Were we supposed to brew up a potion?"

If we didn't need faery blood to transform before, there could've been a number of different ways. My mind never thought I'd have to be injected with the blood of my own kind.

"How did you come into possession of so much fae blood?"

"Donations from those who wanted to support our cause."

How did others know about this cure when so many did not? "Which is what, exactly? Your men weren't very forthcoming with information."

"Isn't it obvious? Sharing powers, equal opportunities between our species. If we have the same powers, there will be no need for us to rely on the fae. We'll be able to fend for ourselves. Heal one another; grow crops as efficiently; protect ourselves. The fae will no longer have to take care of the rest of our realm. They'll be free of us."

"So, this will change you as well? This isn't simply a selfless act to allow those of us who wanted to change back, but couldn't, the opportunity to do so."

"It is a little bit of both." His tone was persuasive, indulging even. Too glib for my taste.

I ignored the pit in my stomach. Before I could talk myself out of it, I nodded so Guthron would proceed with shoving the needle into my heart.

"Will you have to use two of these on me as well?"

"You are different than Tarron, so you'll only need one. It will sting a bit for a few moments, but it will be over soon," Guthron coached and positioned the needle over my chest. Fear clawed at my insides. And then, the syringe punctured my skin. Flames lit my veins before I went limp. I fell to the ground.

It felt like I'd been put under anesthesia and was trying to come to, like when I'd had to get my wisdom teeth removed. My brain was in a horrible fog. I couldn't think. I couldn't talk. I couldn't open my eyes. Through the dark I heard faint voices.

"Her ears grew back normally."

"I see her wings are starting to unfurl. They appear to be a normal size."

"Did her eyes grow larger yet?"

"She's getting more color in her skin."

I couldn't feel any of that. My entire body was numb. If I opened my mouth, gibberish would tumble out.

"She'll need a few more moments to wake up. Then we'll know the full extent of her changes."

I didn't understand. What changes? I'd changed? *Wait.* Fae changes. I couldn't feel them yet. But more importantly, why wouldn't they know the full extent of my changes? Wasn't I supposed to return to my original fae form?

When I pried my eyes open, they locked with a familiar set of forest green eyes. *Marcus?* I blinked. That couldn't have been right. My vision cleared, and, sure enough, Marcus's hulking frame stood next to Guthron like they were old buddies.

What was he doing here? I nearly asked when he faintly shook his head once and his eyes narrowed, silencing me. Did he not want them to know we knew each other?

"How are you feeling?" Guthron asked.

My throat was dry, so I swallowed to answer. How *was* I feeling? I closed my eyes and took inventory. Nothing ached. I reached further inside. If anything, I felt stronger. I was in my own skin again. I moved to sit up and hands reached around to steady me.

"I'm fine." I shifted away from the touch. "Just give me some space, would you? I can't think with you breathing down my neck."

"Her feistiness has not faded," Guthron grumbled.

Comfort I'd been waiting to experience for months soothingly wrapped around my body, hugging me. *I've missed you, too, Wings.* I sighed my relief.

"Lia," Marcus asked, "Are you okay? Does anything feel strange?"

I peered up at him standing beside me. "Should I feel strange?"

His mouth opened and closed. Did he not know how to answer my question? Why did he look so anxious?

"No," Guthron answered. "You should feel normal. Your powers should have been restored. Your wings and ears have returned, as have your eyes. Physically, you look as you should."

"So, internally, you want to know if the blood worked."

Marcus nodded. He appeared to be more concerned than anyone else, and I wanted to know why.

I closed my eyes again and focused on the dirt at my feet, sensing the elements in the earth, making them work for me. When I opened my eyes, flowers bloomed along the base of the rock slab they'd placed me on to recover.

"Fascinating," Guthron uttered.

"Is this not the result you were expecting?"

"You're the first to recover and use your power," Marcus said.

"What about Tarron? Shouldn't he have woken up by now?"

Marcus exchanged a look with Guthron. What was he hiding from me? Marcus answered, against what I could assume were Guthron's orders. Why was Marcus listening to Guthron?

"Tarron did not wake up," Marcus said.

THIRTY ONE

SARAI

We watched the elves' hideout, camouflaged high up in a tree, to assess the surrounding area and their defenses.

"They have four guards on duty," Kai said as he counted the elves outside the cave opening. "Declan and I can take them out. After that, Kayne, you and the rest of your men step in and follow Declan and me inside. We want to remain as quiet as possible to catch them off guard. If Marcus is on our side, by the time we get in there, he'll have the upper hand on Guthron."

"And if he's not?" I had to be realistic. Marcus could have lied to me again.

"Then, if we don't make it out with the blood and the scroll within fifteen minutes, Calliope, you and Sarai come in to use your elements. You may need to wipe out all of the elves to keep this contained."

"Minutes?" I asked.

Calliope answered, "I've been teaching Kai how to keep time the only way I know how. I'll let you know when or if we need to go in."

"What, are they vampires?" Cameron asked, his eyes wide as he studied the elves standing guard. "Look at those teeth! They could shred us to pieces with one bite."

"Cam, shhh …" Calliope scolded.

Kai secured his bow and arrow across his back and perched on the edge of the branch, preparing to leap. "Let's go, Dec."

Cameron looked ready to jump out of the tree after Declan and Kai.

"What do you think you're doing?" Calliope grabbed the back of his shirt, holding him in place.

"Lia's probably in there. I'm going in after her."

"And what makes you think you're going to be able to do anything against all these powerful creatures?"

"I've got a knife. I know how to use it. And I've been taking kickboxing classes. My side kick is impeccable."

"Nuh uh, Karate Kid. Not happening." She looped her arm through his, locking him to her side.

He wriggled to get loose to no avail. Cameron groaned and sat down on the bough. "Sometimes I hate being human," he mumbled.

Calliope shushed him again as we watched Kai and Declan approach the cave. Silently and swiftly, they took out the guards one-by-one. Two arrows from Kai took down two, and the third was brought down by Declan with a snapped neck. The guards didn't stand a chance. Though, I wished it could've been done without violence, I immediately felt more confidence in the situation. With their speed, and Marcus on the inside, they'd be in and out in no time.

"What's taking them so long?" I paced the limb.

"It's only been five minutes, Sarai," Calliope said.

"I don't know what that means."

"You'll have to wait twice as long before you and I need to go in. Don't worry. Kai and Declan are the best Keepers in Faylinn. Plus, four of your Keepers are backing them up. I have faith they'll succeed."

"We do not know how many elves are in there. How many have changed by now. There could be hundreds. For all we know, Marcus isn't in there and all of our Keepers have been taken down."

"Don't forget as fae we have strength and speed on our side. The elves might be cunning, but we're stronger. There could be a hundred elves in there, and Kai and Declan could take them all out by themselves."

"I am glad you have so much confidence in them, but I do not want to wait any longer. I cannot bear not knowing what is going on inside. There could be slaughter and we wouldn't know."

"Five more minutes. Give them a chance, Sarai. I don't know about you, but I don't want to have to use my elements against the elves. They are no match for you and I together. Not to mention we're not alone out here. Our elements will cause a scene and draw attention. None of us want that."

"All the more reason to go in now and put an end to

this."

Calliope took my shoulders in her hands, forcing me to face her. "You don't want a war, but you're willing to massacre an entire clan of elves?"

I took a deep breath. "I know you are right. I simply worry they've already changed and our Keepers stood no chance, and here we are wasting time, while they die needlessly."

Calliope winced. "Fine," she conceded. "We'll go in, but we won't use our elements unless absolutely necessary. Okay?"

I nodded. "Thank you."

"Cameron, don't you dare move."

"And go where?"

"Good boy."

"Thank you, master."

Calliope shot him an amused look, hugged him, and then dove off the branch.

I followed close behind as we snuck into the dim cave. Torches lit our path, but didn't shed nearly enough light. The cave was unsettlingly quiet. Where were the voices? The fighting? We should have been able to detect something by now.

Calliope pulled the bow and an arrow from her back and held it in position. I slipped a dagger from the sheath at my ankle and crept up beside her. We were a team. I didn't want her standing in front of me, as though I needed protection. We'd had the same teacher once. We were equals.

The tunnel stretched on, growing wider and wider. Would it ever end? Gradually, voices echoed off the stone walls. We hugged the rock, searching behind us as we approached, making sure no one was sneaking up on us.

A booming voice traveled down the tunnel from the direction we were headed. "Did you really think a few Keepers could come in and stop us? It is quite laughable. We have a Royal on our side. One word and he could take you all out at once."

I swallowed my gasp. They were using Marcus as their muscle? The passageway opened up into a giant space with all of our Keepers tied up in the center, surrounded by a thousand, if not more, angry elves.

"So powerful you have a Royal doing your dirty work, Guthron?" Kai taunted. "I'd say *that's* quite laughable."

"Thank you for volunteering," Guthron said, stopping in front of Kai. He placed the tip of his sword at Kai's throat. "You're first to go, faery."

"Oh, no he isn't," Calliope hissed and walked out into the cavern, her bow and arrow poised and ready to shoot. "Hey Guthron! You probably should've thought twice before messing with my husband."

Guthron's head whipped around. His lip curled up. "Queen Calliope, what a lovely surprise."

"Isn't it? If you would be so kind as to untie my men, I'd appreciate it."

He clicked his tongue. "I am afraid I cannot oblige. You see, they came into my territory and attacked my men. There must be consequences."

"Oh, I'll give you consequences." Calliope's arrow flew across the room, into our group of Keepers. Her arrow grazed the twine tied around Kai's wrists and he sprung free. Swiftly, he pulled a dagger from his footwear and slit the rope off the rest before crouching, ready to strike.

"It is amusing that you think you can stop us," Guthron

sneered.

"And it is amusing that you think we cannot." I walked out of the tunnel and took my place by Calliope with my dagger ready to fight.

"And Queen Sarai, my my. This is quite the surprise. I hoped you and I would have a different meeting. Either way, there is a small detail you two might not be aware of. I have a Royal you might know. Marcus, come say hello."

Marcus stepped away from the shadows behind Guthron into the dim lighting. His massive figure adorned and pierced with bone towered above the lanky elf. I had never seen his eyes look so menacing, and they were not aimed at the enemy. They were trained on Calliope and me. Internally, I shrank back, but I held my ground and stared back. At the man I thought I could love.

"Dispose of them please," Guthron ordered.

Marcus stalked toward Calliope and me, his cloak fanning out behind him as he pursued. Maybe I was right about his true allegiance. I didn't want to be, but how else had they been able to capture all of the Keepers in a matter of minutes? Unless he'd warned them. We'd played right into his hand.

"I did not want it to turn out this way," he said, his pace not slowing. "I tried to find another way, but you made it impossible. You came too close to succeeding. I have to make this right."

My heart shattered. I was right. I was going to have to fight Marcus. My fist tightened around the dagger.

"Lia, run!" Marcus shouted. Lia appeared in full fae form from where Marcus had stood behind Guthron. "Get out of here now!"

Lia bolted across the expanse, faltering as she passed us.

She stopped only momentarily to nod at us before she barreled down the darkened tunnel. As soon as she was gone, Marcus spun away from us and fire shot from the torches, searing the elves closest to the flames. Their screams filled the cavern.

"Go after her!" Guthron shouted at his clan. "Don't let her get away!"

Calliope shot arrows at every elf that attempted to follow Lia. My dagger wasn't going to be nearly as effective as I'd hoped. Sheathing it at my ankle, I honed in on the water beneath the surface. Before any more elves could attempt their escape, a geyser shield of water shot up, blocking the exit. Every elf trying to pass was hurled at the ceiling by the force of the water.

Marcus stood between Calliope and me, hands twitching at his sides, ready to aim fire.

"It appears there are three Royals against you, Guthron!" I yelled. "We do not want to fight. We will show you mercy. All we want is the scroll, the blood, and a promise this will stop."

His maniacal laughter ricocheted throughout the cavern. "That will never happen. Samras! Ardis! Nevin!"

Three elves emerged from the horde. They stood taller than the rest, had more muscle than the rest. Their ears weren't nearly as sharp, nor were their teeth. Calliope's arrows sailed through the air and impaled each of them, but they were unfazed. They pulled the arrows from their bleeding chests and pressed on with entertained sneers.

"These three were the successful experiments who drank our blood," Marcus quickly explained. "They are stronger, smarter, and nearly unaffected by pain. They heal rapidly, and they are *fast*."

Before I could conjure up water, my head slammed against the cave wall. A hand clamped around my throat and rocks sharply dug into my back. Steely eyes bore into mine. I couldn't swallow. I couldn't breathe. My feet dangled above the ground. I clawed at the hand gripping my neck, but it was futile. Darkness was encroaching on my vision.

Someone shouted, "Let her go!"

Everything went black.

THIRTY TWO

CAMERON

Sigh.

I felt so useless. Once again. My friends were fighting for their lives while I hid for my own safety. I wanted to be able to stand beside them, help them. I needed to get bit by a radioactive spider or struck by a lightning bolt. Maybe I could convince the government to experiment on me. Something was bound to give me supernatural powers, so I could hold my own in this world.

A figure stumbled out of the mouth of the cave, and I pressed my back against the rough bark of the trunk to remain invisible. Peering around the side, my eyes zeroed in on red hair. Lia? Wings stretched out of her back as her head whipped up. Her recognizable eyes searched the forest.

LIA! I almost shouted her name, but if she was escaping I couldn't draw attention to her. Pushing off the trunk, I stood in the middle of the broad limb, jumping up and down, and waved my arms to catch her attention. In hushed tones I shout-whispered her name. I felt like one of the three amigos, standing on the cement wall, making birdcalls. *Look up here! Look up here!*

Before she darted in another direction, our eyes connected. Her head knocked to the side like she was wondering if she was imagining me. In an instant, she was on the limb beside me.

"What in the ever-living heck are you doing in Faylinn?"

"Looking for you! What does it look like? What happened to you? You're … a faery again."

Her voice quieted. "They changed me."

"I can see that."

Lia was a faery again. It finally clicked. We stared at each other, wordlessly. What it meant for Lia being a faery again burrowed into my brain like a tick. She wouldn't be coming back with me.

"I didn't really think it through," she said.

"You left without saying goodbye."

"It was kind of one of those, this-deal-expires-as-soon-as-we-walk-away deals, so I reacted on impulse."

Right. Of course. She was able to be a faery again. Why wouldn't she jump on that opportunity? This was her true world. That shouldn't hurt me. Why was I so hurt? It wasn't personal. She wasn't specifically choosing to leave me. I was just an unfortunate casualty.

For the first time in my life, I didn't know what to say.

Lia opened her mouth to—what I could only assume was—let me down gently, but her eyes shifted over my shoulder and panic engulfed them. "Cameron, get down!" She shoved me to the side, causing me to lose my balance and fall to the forest floor.

With the wind knocked out of me, I stared up at the branches swaying above me from my back, black spots floating in my line of sight. I couldn't do anything but blink and try to figure out what had happened. Did Lia just push me out of the tree? I couldn't feel my arms or my legs. Was I paralyzed? *I cannot get paralyzed right now.*

Lying on my back, my eyes traveled up the trunk until I saw Lia still in the tree, fighting one of the creepy fanged guys. I couldn't call them elves. Elves were happy and smiley and worked in Santa's workshop. These things were what nightmares were made of.

Somewhere in the back of my mind I knew I should move and hide, but I couldn't. My body was out of commission. *Seriously. Am I paralyzed?* I fell like thirty feet. If not paralyzed, something had to be broken.

I could only move my eyes. They watched Lia and her ninja skills against vampire face. A kick to the abdomen. A punch to the jaw. A block to keep him from nailing her face. I watched as she ran up the trunk, back flipped and twisted in the air, roundhouse kicking Vampire Face in the jaw, knocking him off the tree. Which was good in theory; except he landed beside me. And I still couldn't move.

I heard a thud on the ground near the other side of my body. *Please be Lia. Please be Lia.*

"Cameron, move!" she barked.

Didn't she realize I would've done that already if I could? "You nearly killed me by pushing me out that tree, and now you think I'm just laying here for the heck of it?"

Without a retort, Lia swept me up in her arms, placed me

against a tree farther out of the way and sped back to finish off the elf. Faery speed never ceased to catch me off guard.

Propped up, I saw Vampire Face was already closing in on her, his long nails spread out like Wolverine. Feeling began to make its way back into my extremities, and I edged closer to a shrub with my right elbow to better conceal myself. If I was useless as a human with a knife, I was even more useless as a *wounded* human with a knife. I was almost ninety-nine-point-nine percent sure my left arm was broken.

No matter what moves Lia used on Vampire Face, he came back for more, stronger and angrier than before. He was a resilient thing. As fascinating as it was to watch her kick his trash, she wasn't going to win this fight with her ninja skills. No matter how awesome they were. I fished the knife from its sheath on my hip Calliope gave me.

"Lia!" *Please let her reflexes be as good as her ninja skills.* "Catch!"

The knife went sailing through the air. Flipping back to catch my poor aim, Lia snagged the hilt like a champ. With one swipe to the throat, Vampire Face went down. Lia crouched, scanning the forest for more before she darted to me.

"Are you okay?"

"I'm not paralyzed, so that's a bonus, but I'm pretty sure my arm is broken." I cradled it against my chest.

"I'm sorry." She placed her palm on my cheek. "I didn't mean to push you out of the tree. I mean, I did, but I didn't think we were that far up. The elf was coming at your back, and I reacted. I'm so sorry."

She'd been reacting quickly a lot lately. So, I followed her lead. I grabbed the back of her neck with my good hand and pressed my mouth to hers. Kissing Lia made the pain in my left arm ebb. Mostly because the pain traveled to my heart. She was a faery, and I was a human. And we were never going to be. But, dang it all, I was going to kiss her, as much as I could until I would no longer get the chance.

Lia pulled back and rested her forehead against mine. "I'm so sorry." If I didn't know any better, I'd say I heard tears in Lia's voice.

"It's okay," I whispered, keeping my hand tangled in her hair. "I get it. You don't have to apologize."

"We're not finished with you, Faery."

She reared back. Three vampire faces surrounded us, looming menacingly. Lia reached back and covertly placed the knife in my good hand. "You might need this," she whispered under her breath.

Oh crap.

The vampire faces converged on us. Lia took two, while the third fixated on me. Ignoring the pain coursing through my body, I managed to get up and stood in the defensive pose my instructor had taught me. His jagged teeth gleamed and his nails spread like talons. Were those things retractable?

I'm in trouble.

"You know, Human, we could change you, too." Was he bargaining with me? Also, was he for real or trying to distract me?

"There might be a few interesting side-effects, but you wouldn't have to be a weak human anymore." The corners of his mouth turned up. If he was trying to smile at me, he was doing a very poor job.

"I think I'll pass. Thanks."

"Suit yourself." Vampire Face lunged at me, and I spun away, nearly face-planting as I lost my balance. Falling out of that tree was not helping my odds. At least I was enough of a distraction to keep Lia from fighting off three of these things.

"You're not very agile on your feet, Human."

"And you're awfully frightening to look at," I countered.

He sneered and swiped his hand through the air. This time I wasn't quick enough. His claw-like nails sliced through my left arm I held up in defense.

"Watch it with those nails! You really should get them trimmed. Maybe a little manicure? I hear chicks dig that kind of thing."

"Enough talking and more fighting," he roared, coming at me again.

With every swipe of my knife, he dodged left and right, and then advanced once more. I couldn't even knick him. I kept backing away, but never far enough. I attempted my impeccable side kick and failed. I had cuts all over my body. I was losing stamina. One wrong step and I was a dead man.

An explosion erupted inside the cave. Vampire Face made one mistake. He looked over his shoulder, and that was my opening. One slash across the throat was all I needed, and he went down.

I'm one lucky son of a gun.

Looking down, I saw a hand gripping the hilt of a bloody knife. Was that my hand? My fingers unlatched their grasp, dropping the knife. Vampire Face's lifeless body lay at my feet, surrounded in red liquid. I backed away. What did I just do?

My fingers latched on the roots of my hair. I scoured the land, searching for Lia, expecting to see her leaning against a trunk with her arms crossed, taunting me. *Can't win a little fight with an elf, Cameron?* She was nowhere. Out of the corner of my eye, red hair splayed across the forest floor, tangled in vines and dried leaves caught my attention. And two dead elves lay at her feet.

"Lia!" I scrambled to her side, my knees scraping across the dirt and grit. Had I been able to feel more than concern for Lia, my knees would most likely be stinging, rubbed raw by the earth. Not to mention the slices all over my body. I couldn't focus on those. Turning her to face me, I brushed the tousled hair from her face. "Lia, are you okay?"

My eyes spotted crimson pooling on her bare stomach, the material torn away. She groaned and placed her hand over it, capturing the blood, trying to close the gash. "Cameron," she whispered, "I'm not strong enough to heal myself. Take my blood."

"What?"

"Take it," she choked and placed one hand on top of the other. "I protected it. I can close my wound enough to save it for you. Just take it. Transform."

"Are you insane? What are you talking about? I can't transform. Don't be stupid."

"Yes, you can," she croaked. "I mean it."

"Stop being so self-sacrificing. I don't want your blood. I want you to live." I placed my hands on top of hers to add pressure to stop the bleeding. "Calliope!" I shouted into the night. I didn't know if she could hear me from the cave, but I needed her to help heal Lia. Screw the elves!

"You know the human world no longer holds your interest. This is the perfect out. No one innocent has to die."

"No one innocent?" I snorted, choking on my pained laughter. "This whole martyr act is getting old, Lia. You paid for your sins with your life when you changed Kai back. I think you've sacrificed enough."

"But you can be in this world with Calliope and live a long life with Sarai." Lia took an unsteady breath and tried to swallow.

"I've lived without Calliope before. I don't need her to survive. And I don't love Sarai."

"You might change your mind."

"No! Be quiet!" I gripped Lia's arms. I wanted to shake her. Instead, I placed my hands over hers, adding more pressure to her bleeding wound. "I don't want Sarai, okay?"

Her eyes scoured my face, emotions flickering across like wings. Confusion. Fear. Hope?

"Are you that stupid and hard-headed?" I placed one red-smeared hand gently on her cheek. "I love *you*, you idiot."

Lia shook her head, a tear escaping down her temple onto the soil. Was she denying me? Did she not believe me? I knew it was a little out of the blue, but after that kiss, how could she not feel it?

"I don't need this world. I just need you." Lia's eyes fluttered closed. I frantically searched through the trees. "Calliope! Sarai! Anyone!"

"Cameron, stop," she murmured.

"No, you stop! I understand why you came back. This is your world, where you belong. You earned this blood back. Stop squandering your life. Stop thinking you don't deserve it!"

Her head shook. "We could never be together anyway. If I survive, I stay here. I can't go back with you. At least this way one of us can be happy."

"This is ridiculous. We'd figure it out. Stop talking. Save your energy." I lifted my gaze, combing through the shrubbery. "Calliope! Calliope!" My voice sounded gravelly to my own ears. I was losing force. "Help me, please!" I cried.

"It's no use, Cameron. No one is coming. They have a bigger battle to fight in there."

"Yes, they are, dang it. Calliope!"

"Cameron, shut up!" Lia choked and coughed. "Just shut up and kiss me."

I shook my head. Kissing her meant I was accepting this. It meant saying goodbye. I refused to say goodbye to Lia.

"You'd deny a girl her dying wish?"

I leaned down, unsmiling. I wouldn't laugh at her attempt to joke with me. "I'm not kissing you because this is over. I'm kissing you because I want to. You're not dying. Stay with me."

"Staying," she said in a faded whisper as her eyes fluttered close. I pressed my lips to hers, but her mouth didn't react to mine.

"Lia." I pulled away to look at her. Her head fell to the side, slack. "Lia?" I shook her, but she didn't respond. "Lia!"

THIRTY THREE

SARAI

I pried my eyes open, but everything was a blur. I knew I was lying down. The earth was rough beneath my shoulder and side. "Sarai," someone said. "Can you hear me? Sarai, are you okay?"

My eyes clenched shut. There was too much. Too much pain. Too many sounds. Too many figures. Too many things fighting for my attention.

"Sarai, *please* say something. Can you hear me?"

I took a deep breath and opened my eyes again. Marcus's concerned face came into focus. "Are you all right?"

"I will be," I croaked. Beyond Marcus, pandemonium unfurled throughout the cavern. Calliope took out several elves at once with a gust of wind, knocking them against the wall. While our Keepers dominated with strength and speed. This was not what I'd wanted. Why couldn't Guthron see reason?

Tears filled my eyes as I tried to sit up.

"Be careful," he urged and helped prop me against the rock. "Can you still use your element?"

I nodded. If I had to use it sitting down, I would. This would end one way or another. If I had to take them all out with a tsunami, I would. As soon as the Keepers and Calliope and Marcus were safe, I would flood this entire cave.

Marcus peered at me with the saddest eyes, his hand cradling my face. I was about to tell him to leave me and fight when one of the enhanced elves appeared behind Marcus, arm raised with a sword above his head.

"Marcus, watch out!"

With rapid speed, Marcus rolled out of the way and the sword came down between my legs, nearly severing my knee. My eyes shot up and met the elf's frightening glare. He hissed and heaved the sword back, prepared to take my life. Fire blasted from the torch above me and engulfed the elf's face. He stumbled back and ran into the chaos, trying to slap out the fire.

Marcus grabbed my hand and pulled me to my feet. I scanned the sides of the cave and spotted a ledge near the top. "Get us to higher ground."

"What?"

"We need to get to that ledge." I pointed. "All of us. We need to tell Calliope and the Keepers. I have a plan."

"But, we need to secure the scroll and the blood first."

"Where are they being kept?" I asked.

"I don't know, but Guthron must be storing the blood near by. He changed Lia here in the cavern, and the blood needed to stay fresh long enough for the transfer."

I did not want to think of how fresh it needed to be. "I

will find it. Just get them to that ledge, and I will meet you up there."

Marcus hesitated, his gaze memorizing my face. For a beat of my heart he held my stare. I realized my hand was still locked in his grasp. I hadn't bothered to twist free. "Be careful, Sarai. *Please*," he said before he charged the mob of elves and joined the fight.

I leaped across from wall to wall above the throng, until I reached the ledge and searched for another tunnel or crevasse where Guthron could have a den or some place to hide the scroll and blood. On the opposite end of the cavern, a smaller opening appeared to lead down the other end of the cave. I flipped down and bolted for the break in the wall. Before I could go any farther, Guthron blocked my path, standing in the middle of the opening with his sword ready to strike.

"This way, unfortunately, is off limits." His answer gave away the position of what I wanted. Poor decision on his part.

"Guthron, this can end now. No one else has to die. Hand over the scroll and the blood, and we can agree on a ceasefire."

"That will never happen. We were given the scroll. It is rightfully ours to do as we please."

Given the scroll? "By who? No one would willingly give it up. No one even knew of its existence. It belongs to the True Royal family of Faylinn."

"And now it belongs to us. You have your brother to thank for that.

My brother?

"Skye made sure it wound up in the right hands."

"Skye?" I choked. He was misguided, but to turn on his own kind. It made no sense. "He would never."

"You think your brother worshipped your father and believed in his cause?" Guthron laughed. "He didn't think your father could follow through and force the other kingdoms to live in Faylinn. We were supposed to build an army to make the rest of the kingdoms comply, and in return we would receive your powers. He called for a truce. You did us a favor by taking out Skye *and* Adair. We owe no one now."

My family's transgressions would never stop haunting me. "You must see how dangerous the information in that scroll is. That scroll holds the key to our existence."

"And ironically enough, that power now resides in my hands."

I angled myself to look over my shoulder at the carnage piling up. With the power of their elements, Marcus and Calliope were taking out numerous amounts of elves at once. One sweep of my hand, and the rest could be annihilated.

"The last thing I want is to fight fire with fire. Let us work this out civilly. I believe we can still live in peace." I had to believe. Otherwise, there would never be accord again.

"We have been oppressed for long enough!" he seethed. "We deserve your powers. We are not a pawn to be played."

"Of course you're not. You are free to do whatever you choose in this world. No one is stopping you. But, killing innocent fae to obtain their powers will not be tolerated. Turn over the scroll and the blood, and this will all be over. You can go back to living in peace, and so shall we. We will put this behind us."

"There is no peace, Sarai," he scoffed. "The elves have always been feared, shunned, avoided. We are deprived of our own kingdom, forced to share the land and move when our dwelling is no longer habitable for our protection. Pixies do not require the space we do, the mermaids own every body of water, and the trolls are too dense to know they deserve more. If I return the scroll to you, we are left with nothing to our advantage."

I needed to find a solution. One that ended the violence and concealed what happened here. The more contained, the better. "I am a reasonable woman, Guthron. I am not my father, or my brother, Skye." I may be a Royal, but I was not above begging. "What do you want? If it is within my means, I will make it happen. What will keep you from further pursuing this?"

"You want to bargain with me?" Guthron appeared confused by my willingness to negotiate. Had we truly never treated them as equals?

"I want this to end. I am tired of death and loss. I am tired of war and anger. I want us to live in a world where there is peace and understanding. I want to amend my father's wrongs and give back the lives that were taken advantage of."

His chest puffed out as he stood taller, attempting to intimidate me. "I want our own kingdom, a branch on the Waking Oak."

I frowned. "That is not up to me, Guthron. You know that. The Waking Oak creates as it sees fit. If it were up to me, I would give that to you."

"Then you have nothing to offer me."

"If you do not give me something, every last one of you will die."

"This sounds less like a negotiation and more like a threat."

"It is a fact. I cannot allow you to continue slaughtering my fae, and you cannot afford to lose any more of yours. And rest assured, if you refuse to cease, not one of your fellow men will remain when I am through with you. If we come to an agreement, no one else has to die."

"Your blood is the only thing I want."

"And I cannot let you have it."

Think, Sarai. Think. I spared a glace at the battle behind me as it continued on. There seemed to be more on the ground than those who remained standing and fighting. Was this what it looked like at the Battle of Faylinn? Did anyone show mercy?

I spun back to him. "What if I give you a portion of Rymidon? Miles and miles of land for you to call your own. It's not your own kingdom, but it is more than enough for the number of you that is left. You will not have to continue relocating. Rymidonian craftsmen will help you build homes and whatever you might need. You will have access to our harvests and our trade with other kingdoms. My Keepers will also serve as protection. An attack on the elves will be an attack on me. I will be your advocate. If there is anything you need—anything within reason—I will do what I can to help."

Guthron blinked, either unable to fathom my offer or contemplating my seriousness. I could tell my offer was more than he'd received in the past. How cruelly had my father treated them for our kinds to hate each other so intensely, to be mortal enemies?

"I am showing you mercy, Guthron. Take it. In exchange for your silence and the ceasing of transformations, I will grant you all of this. Hand over the blood and the scroll, and this ends now. The fighting ends today."

Guthron's mouth pinched in consideration. He held up his hand and shouted, "Stadeb!" His booming voice echoed throughout the cavern. I had no idea what it meant, but every elf immediately ceased their fighting and looked to Guthron.

"I have one more condition," I said. "You must all remain in Rymidon, no traveling to other kingdoms. You will be free to roam our land, but if you must travel through the Waking Oak, you will be accompanied by one of my Keepers. I need the assurance that all fae are safe, that there will be no other kingdoms targeted. If you prove yourselves trustworthy, we can renegotiate these terms in the future, but until then, this is what I ask of you."

A hand gripped my shoulder. Calliope whispered in my ear, "Are you sure you know what you're doing?"

I nodded once. This was my decision. Calliope wasn't going to change my mind.

"He could turn on you at any point," she tried to reason.

I murmured, "And the repercussions will be tenfold."

Guthron hesitated before he outstretched his hand. His sharp nails gave me pause, but I needed to trust him. I needed him to know I trusted him. I placed my hand around his wrist and his fingers locked around mine in a root.

"We will agree to your terms."

Internally, I heaved a sigh, but kept my outward appearance reserved. "This agreement is binding. I am a fair woman, but I will not be exploited. If you or any of your clan breaks this treaty, everything I have offered will be taken away. There will be severe consequences."

"The same will go for you and your kingdom. If any of the things you promised are withdrawn, the blood of your kind if fair game."

"Then let us remain fair and understanding."

THIRTY FOUR

LIA

Muffled sounds flooded my ears. My brain was in too much of a haze to place my surroundings. I tried to open my eyes, but my lids felt like they'd been cemented shut.

"C'mon, Lia. Wake up. Wake up, Lia." *Calliope?* "Cameron, her eyes fluttered."

A gentle hand pressed to my jaw, a thumb stroking my cheek. "Lia? I'm here. Come back to me." *Cameron?* "Please come back to me."

What happened to me? Why couldn't I move? I was so uncomfortable. Something ragged dug into my shoulder blade. I shifted away from it.

"No, hold still," Calliope ordered, pressing my shoulders into the ground. "You're still healing."

"It hurts," I muttered.

"I know," she sympathized, "but you have to stay still.

Your wound was so deep. It may take another few minutes for you to feel like yourself."

"No," I groaned, trying to move again. "My shoulder. It hurts."

After a second, I felt them move me to the side, and the sharp pain in my shoulder disappeared. "That's better." I sighed.

Someone laughed. "Good grief. She gets stabbed in the stomach, but she's complaining about a rock in her back."

I opened my eyes. "It really hurt."

Cameron hovered above me and smiled, but his expression was off. "Welcome back."

"Hi." I attempted to smile at him. The pain in my stomach pulsed as it fought to heal. "Did we win?"

"Sarai took care of it," Calliope answered, but she didn't sound convinced.

I looked to her. "I feel like that's not an answer."

"She showed a lot more mercy than I would have, but it's over. The scroll and blood are on their way back to Faylinn with Declan and Kai. They'll be kept in a secure place until we decide what to do with them."

"How long have I been out?"

"Not long," she said. "I came out to a very frantic Cameron. We almost lost you. I showed up with barely enough time. I could feel the life leaving you."

My eyes drifted to Cameron whose emotions finally registered. He looked terrified. "Thank you, Calliope," I said.

"Thank the boy scout here." She patted Cameron on the back. "He held pressure on your wound long enough for me to get to you. You would've bleed out for sure if not for him."

He stayed with me. How long had he stayed, waiting for

me to fade away, thinking I would die? "Thank you, Cameron." I clutched his hand by my side, and all he did was nod.

"We should get back to Faylinn. You need to rest, Lia. And I need to get Cameron back home."

Right. Cameron had to leave. I didn't want Cameron to leave me. *What have I done?*

Calliope showed me to the guest room down the hall from her chambers where I'd stayed before.

"Get some sleep," she said. "It's late. We can talk about what you're going to do in the morning."

"I'll lay down, but could Cameron and I have a minute before you take him back?"

Calliope gave me a funny look. "Okay, but make it quick. He's acting more and more strange. I don't think I can handle Cameron going crazy on top of everything else today."

I nodded, and she left the room. Was he acting more and more strange because he was a human in the faery world? Or was it because he felt as heartbroken as I did?

After a long stretch of quiet, Cameron said, "So."

"So," I said.

He swallowed and dug his hands into his front pockets as he rocked back on his heels. "I guess I'll still get to come to faery parties and we can hang out, so there's that."

"Yes. There's that." I tried to smile, but something told me it didn't look like much of one. I stared down at my feet, thoughts of what I wanted to say to him running around inside my brain, but none of them slowed down long enough or seemed like the right thing to say.

Thanks for taking care of me.

I had fun living with you.

I think I love you, too.

"Would it be blasphemous if I asked Calliope to use some of the left over faery blood on me?"

My head whipped up.

He nervously rubbed his hands together. "I know it's the blood of innocent faeries—or alleged innocent faeries, they could've deserved to die for all we know—but if it's going to be disposed of anyway, what could it hurt, right?"

"Cameron, we don't even know if the blood would work on you." My heart raced rapidly inside of my chest.

"But, it's worth a shot, don't you think?"

Yes.

GLIMMER

THIRTY FIVE

CAMERON

"Are you insane?!"

I knew this conversation wasn't going to go over well.

"What if it doesn't work on you?" Calliope stood in the middle of the atrium with her arms spread wide, looking at me like I was an idiot. Yup. This was the exact reaction I was expecting. "The elves knew the right amount of blood that was needed for them and the amount needed for faeries like Lia after experimenting for months. The chemical make up of your body is completely different, Cam. You're human. Not to mention weight, height—all of that needs to be taken into consideration. What if the dosage of blood is wrong? Then what? You die, Cam. That's what! No. No. You're not changing. I won't allow it."

"I'm not one of your faeries. This isn't your decision, Cal."

181

"It should be!" she yelled. "It's going to be difficult enough as it is to explain how Lia transformed back. *Everyone* would question how you became a faery." Calliope flung her arms in the air, throwing all kinds of hand gestures and sweeping motions between Lia and me. No one talked with her hands more than Callie did. "Faylinn and Rymidon all know you were my *human* best friend. We were trying to keep this under wraps. We do not want anyone else knowing what can be done with our blood."

Solutions ran through my mind. "What if we go to one of the other kingdoms to live?"

"It doesn't work like that, Cam. It's not like moving from city-to-city or state-to-state. You can't just bounce from kingdom-to-kingdom. We don't all work the same. We have different laws and rules. Not to mention, enough rumors have been spread. Everyone knows who Lia is now. She's probably safest in Rymidon."

So, what was I supposed to do? Was I supposed to forget about Lia? Just go back to my life like I hadn't fallen in love again. *Who cares what the human wants? His battles aren't as significant to fight.* Was I being selfish? Yes. I wasn't blind. This was a secret that needed to be kept, but I'd lost too many people in my life. My mom and Calliope were enough. I was supposed to lose Lia now, too? When was I allowed to keep just one piece of happiness?

"And what about your dad?"

"You know we don't have the best relationship. I might as well have lost him at the same time my mom left. He won't miss me. And if I become a faery, he'll forget I even existed, right?"

"There's no way of knowing, Cam. I'm half and half, so

human blood still runs through me. There's no telling if you'll have traces of human blood still or if it'll change you completely. There are too many indefinite variables, and you're willing to risk it all on the chance that your body may or may not accept the change?"

Lia's voice broke through my thoughts. "Calliope has a point, Cameron."

My eyes darted to her. How could she side with her? "Then what? You stay faery and I go back without you? Am I crazy for thinking we had something? Am I alone in this?"

Lia looked like she was about to let me down gently. She opened her mouth to break my heart in two, but Calliope interrupted.

"Wait. You two?" She pointed back and forth between Lia and me. "You two are a thing now?"

Lia and I shared a look. Did I imagine that there was something big here? Something with the power to forever change us. Something strong enough to pull me away from my dad, the only family I had left.

All I did was nod. Lia could deny it if she wanted to, but I knew where I stood and I wanted to fight for it. Lia kept her mouth shut.

"Wow. I was *not* expecting that." Calliope exhaled and walked away from us, her posture tense. From the back I could tell she was pinching the bridge of her nose. This changed everything and we were going to hear all about it.

"*Dang it*, Cameron." She spun around and jabbed her finger at Lia. "And dang it, Lia, for that matter. Why did you have to go and change back? Why would you change back if you wanted to be with him, not knowing if he could change?"

"I… I…" Lia peered over at me. I nearly told her to just

say it already. She didn't love me back. It would make this decision so much easier. And we could stop being scolded by Calliope. "I didn't know. I didn't know I loved him."

Everything stopped. She did? She loved me back? A stupid grin plastered across my face. "You love me, huh?"

Lia shrugged and smiled like she couldn't help herself. "Yeah, dummy. Don't make a big deal out of it." She chewed on her bottom lip.

"You love each other? Like love, love each other." Callie looked at us like we'd officially stumped her. The women had dealt with much more complex situations than this, and her two best friends loving each other was what baffled her?

"I guess so." I grinned from ear-to-ear.

Callie wiped both of her hands down her face with a heavy sigh. "How am I supposed to sit here and prevent you from trying to change, when I pushed every boundary I could to keep Kai?" She groaned and looked like she wanted to stomp her foot. It was good to see she still carried some of her old characteristics. "This is the stupidest idea you've ever had, Cam. I don't like it. I don't like it at all. I hate it. If you die, I will be so mad at you. SO mad." She scowled, and I knew she meant it. If she knew how, she'd bring me back to life just to yell at me and kill me herself. Heck, I'd be mad at myself. I'd survived two faery battles only to die from some faery blood? That would be the lamest death ever. "But I'm a sucker for love."

"Is that a yes?" I asked.

She held up her hands to keep me from getting my hopes up. "I need to talk to Sarai about it first. I don't want her thinking I'm going around using the blood however I choose. This needs to be a collective decision. It affects her, too, if you two will be living in Rymidon."

"Okay." I nodded. "I get that. Can we go with you?"

"I think it's best if I have this conversation alone. I don't want her to be swayed one way or another because of your pitiful puppy dog faces."

"*Hey!*"

Callie laughed. "There are also some other things I want to discuss with her. I'll be back in a couple hours."

After Calliope walked out of the room, leaving Lia and me alone, silence settled between us. Gradually, our gazes met, and, to my surprise, Lia looked nervous. She wasn't far from me, but too far for my liking. I reached out gently drew her to me by her arm.

"So, I know I should be scared, and Sarai could say no or I could die, but I have to tell you something." Slipping an arm around her waist, I lifted the other to her face. "You look pretty hot as a faery."

"As opposed to not being a faery?" She raised her eyebrow.

"Both are favorites," I clarified. "I can just tell this is your true self. Everything beautiful about you as a human intensified. You're more confident in this skin."

Wait a second. Was she blushing?

I pressed my nose to hers and closed my eyes, inhaling deeply. Everything about this felt right. I *should* be scared, but I wasn't. Something told me Calliope would help me figure it out.

"I guess since I haven't said it yet … I love you, too," she whispered and crushed her lips to mine.

THIRTY SIX

SARAI

"And you're okay with this?"

"I'm only okay with it if you are." Calliope stood from sitting on my bed and walked closer to me, sitting on my window seat. "I understand the risks. It puts you in a dangerous position. If anyone finds out what happened, and how Lia was changed back, and how a human changed into a faery ... it could cause serious issues. We'll have to figure out what to tell everyone, but if we get our stories straight, we can make it work. But, again, Sarai, if, for any reason, you are uncomfortable with this, say the word. I will tell Cameron no, and we'll never talk about it again."

The possibilities trickled into my mind. "Calliope, do you realize what else you could do with the blood? Who else you could change if it works?"

She looked at me, apprehensive, like she was holding her

breath. "I've thought about it, but I'm terrified to even change Cameron. Even if the transition worked for my mom, I don't know if living here, allowing her to remember my dad is better than living obliviously without him. She'd have to make that decision. The change would also mean her living longer, and I can't imagine her falling in love again. So, if she changes, she could live that many more years alone."

"But she would have you. Her only family. And when you have children, she'll get to see her grandchildren grow up. Calliope, you could have it all. You could have both worlds. The last two most important people you left behind."

She blinked a couple times. "Are you saying you're okay with Cameron changing?"

I scooted over and pulled her to sit beside me. "Calliope, we have both lost and sacrificed so much. If we have the power to give others happiness, why withhold it? If becoming fae will make Cameron happy, will you make you happy, I have no reservations. The scroll has been returned to its rightful owner. The elves have been silenced. If it comes down to it, we'll get rid of the rest of the blood so it does not fall into the wrong hands. And we will deal with the fallout in our kingdoms if it comes."

"There's no guarantee that we'll use the right amount of blood. There could be serious side effects if we're wrong. Worst-case scenario, he dies."

"That is up to Cameron, is it not?"

"He doesn't have the best decision-making track record. He once rolled down a flight of stairs in a wheelchair just to see if he could do it without falling out."

"What's a wheelchair?"

"It's a chair on wheels that's used to mobilise people who

can't walk."

"Oh. And did he make it?"

"No. He broke his right arm. The entire summer between our sophomore and junior years, I had to listen to him complain about how he couldn't go to the beach or go swimming or do anything with water."

It was difficult to hold in my laughter. "I understand your need to protect him, but ultimately, Cameron is the only one who should decide his fate, don't you think?"

"What are you going to do about Marcus?" It was as though she didn't want to hear my approval, so she brought up the one subject I'd intended to avoid.

"I do not want to talk about him, Calliope." I hoped my tone would be enough to stop her questioning. The mere sound of his name was an arrow straight through my heart.

"Just hear me out for a minute, okay?"

I set my jaw. I did not want to so much as think about him, but I equally wanted to know what she thought was so important for me to hear, what she could possibly say to defend him.

Calliope waited for me to nod before she proceeded, "Honestly, I'm grateful Marcus made that deal with the elves. If *he* hadn't, someone else could have, someone truly evil. Guthron could've gotten away with our blood and created a whole new race before we got to them. So many more fae could've died."

"You're *defending* him?"

She held up her hand as if to fend me off. "What Marcus did was wrong. So wrong. I get that. You have every right to be angry with him, to feel deceived. He lied to you and some of your fae died because of that, but think about it for a minute. His plan was only to get rid of the rest of your father's followers, making the ones responsible for the war pay. He went about it the wrong way, I know, but his intent wasn't entirely malicious. He didn't want innocent faeries to die. If he'd known from the beginning what Guthron had planned, he wouldn't have joined forces. I believe that."

I couldn't look her in the eye anymore, so I looked out my window, still listening, because I knew she was not finished, nor would she stop until she was.

"Do you remember when you were trying to convince me that Sakari was a good man? And you told me not everything is black and white?"

She waited for me to remember the conversation we'd had lifetimes ago in her chambers before they'd bonded. I remembered it vividly. I'd so fiercely wanted her to see the good in Sakari, to grow to love him the way I knew he'd loved her.

"It's true," she continued. "Unfortunately, we deal with a lot of muddled gray areas. Think of the kind of man I once thought Sakari was before I got to know him, and think of the man you knew, the man he actually was." Her words came crashing down. "Could Marcus have handled the situation differently? Yes. Should he have consequences for his actions? Absolutely. I think he's dealing with the fallout right now. He lost you."

When I peered back at her, Calliope had a knowing look.

"Marcus had to watch his best friend—a woman he once loved—die in a war he never should have had to fight, in a war forced upon all of us. While I don't believe vengeance is the answer, I can't say if Skye was standing in front of me that I wouldn't kill him myself for taking away Sakari. It wouldn't bring Sakari back, but at least the person responsible would receive equivalent punishment. If that makes me a terrible faery, so be it."

Then it would make me a terrible faery, as well, because I could almost forgive Marcus for letting those men die. Dare I say they'd deserved it if they'd stood behind my father without pause, but this was more. It was personal.

"Are you saying I am supposed to forgive him? I opened my heart and trusted in him, trusted that he was on my side, and the entire time he was against me. I was beginning to fall in love with him, Calliope! I feel like a fool!"

Her bottom lip quivered, and she bit it. "I know." She nodded as tears welled in her eyes. "I shouldn't defend him, but Marcus didn't know you when the arrangement was made with Guthron. He was fueled by hate and revenge that dissipated the longer he spent time with you. He got to know you, and you softened his heart."

"How do you know that?"

She ignored my question. In the end, he made the right decision because of you. He owned up to his mistakes. He came clean, and that couldn't have been easy to do, knowing there was a risk of losing you."

I didn't tell her any of this before, so the only conclusion I drew was that she'd spoken to him.

"He could've let the elves finish what they started, and then fought them on our side, pretending he never had anything to do with them. Instead, Marcus facilitated putting a stop to a nearly fatal catastrophe that would've affected our entire race." Calliope's hands gently gripped my shoulders. "I'm not telling you to forgive him. If I was in your shoes, I can't say I would be able to, but at least talk to him. Give him a second chance. You are a better person … err … faery than I am.

"Have you spoken to him?"

She looked sheepish. "Marcus may or may not have sought me out before he went back to Oraelia. He knows he doesn't deserve your forgiveness, but he hoped there was something he could do to make it right, to earn back your trust."

"And his plan was to have my sister talk me into it? Very courageous of him."

Calliope shook her head. "This is all me. I truly believe he made a split second decision while he was in a bad place, mentally, that got him in over his head, and he didn't know how to put a stop to it on his own."

"If those are *his* decision making skills, I'm not sure I want someone like him ruling Rymidon beside me."

"Maybe not," Calliope said, thoughtful. "But you're allowing the elves—the ones who facilitated this attack—to live in Rymidon. You offered them resources and shelter and protection." She paused. "And yet, you can't forgive Marcus for lying when he was doing what he thought was just?"

"That is not fair, Calliope. I made a sacrifice by letting the elves have part of my land. I did that to protect the lives of every other faery, to keep that scroll a secret, to keep it from getting into the hands of any other possible enemy. I showed mercy so we weren't forced to kill the entire elf race and suffer the consequences."

"You're right." She nodded with a frown. "You made a split second decision for what you thought was best." Calliope waited, letting her words penetrate the barrier surrounding my heart. *Am I being hypocritical?* "Just speak with Marcus. Give him one more chance to explain himself, to ask for forgiveness. Show him mercy."

THIRTY SEVEN

LIA

"So…" Calliope scanned the open scroll on her desk. It was a lot bigger than I'd imagined. "The scroll doesn't tell us the best way to introduce the blood into your veins or how much to use. It does say why they needed the entire body drained. Apparently, there are different cells in the blood stream that needed to be extracted from the blood of the entire body."

"The jerks told me the blood was donated," I muttered. It'd felt wrong when Guthron said it, but I'd wanted to believe it were true.

Evan, Faylinn's Officiant and Calliope's closest confidant, stood behind her. "The purpose of the scroll was not to teach us how to change others. It was meant to provide the Royals with the knowledge that it was possible, but not recommended, due to the risks." His eyes narrowed on Cameron. "You are aware of the risks."

"Yeah, I am. Calliope won't shut up about them."

Evan's mouth hung open, and his eyes bulged out of his head. He looked like Cameron had just disrespected his mother.

"It needs to be injected straight into his heart," I said. "I'm assuming, because it's the organ that pumps the blood to the rest of the body."

"And how did they do that to you?" Calliope looked like she didn't actually want the answer.

"You're not going to like this," I said to Cameron. "But the fae blood will begin healing you almost immediately."

"Oh no," Calliope groaned. "What did they do to you?"

"They used an instrument that looked like a very large syringe, kind of like when doctors use those adrenaline shots."

"And Guthron just stabbed you in the chest?" Calliope scowled.

"Yeah, pretty much sums it up." I shrugged.

"And you let him do that to you?" she screeched.

"I didn't have much of a choice, and I'd watched them perform the procedure on another who began healing almost as soon as the blood was in his system, so I knew I would be okay."

Calliope folded her arms, her legs spread, taking a superhero stance. "The more I learn, the less I want to let you do this, Cam."

"It's going to be fine, Callie. I think you're worrying for nothing."

"We don't have a large syringe. I don't even know how to get something like that."

"What's a syringe?" Kai asked.

"It's a tube that has a needle on one end and a plunger on the other that pushes the liquid in the tube through the end of the needle," Calliope explained.

"A stellvial?" Evan offered.

"I'd need to see it to know," Calliope said.

Kai made his way to the door of the atrium. "I'll see if Declan and I can obtain one."

"How much blood was used, do you know?" Calliope asked me.

"I wasn't counting the ounces or anything. It could have been five or six, maybe? They used double on Tarron, but he didn't survive."

"If you're going to condone this, you have to give me something better than five or six. Maybe?" Calliope mimicked me. "And a failed attempt amount."

"Trust me," I said through gritted teeth. "I know how crucial it is to get this right. I saw the man before me die, so I'm just as skeptical about this as you are. I'm trying to help." I took a deep breath to calm down. "It didn't take gallons. They didn't do an entire blood transfusion on me. Cameron can't be much different from me since I was human when they changed me."

"But, you were once fae," Calliope argued. "You still had traces of fae blood in your veins, hibernating."

"Actually," Evan said, and we all looked to him. "If I might interject. Because that was Lia's last change, all traces of fae blood had vanished from her veins. That is why we can only change a certain number of times. We are weakened with each transformation. Once the last change occurs, the fae in us can no longer survive."

"Well, if I was full human, then why did I still feel a pull to the forest? How come I still remembered everything?"

"I do not have the answers for that. Fae magic works in mysterious ways. It's possible that because you were originally fae, the veil between our worlds was still thin enough for you to remember. Or it's also possible because Calliope has kept a prominent presence in your lives, it's kept the fae world alive. I cannot give you definite answers, only theories."

"So, what you're saying is the same amount that was used on Lia, could work for me."

Evan's lips pressed into a straight line. "It's a theory, not an solution. We're forcing the change. It's not happening naturally. You may still react differently. It may not kill you, but there could be some undesirable side effects."

"Tell me something I don't know," Cameron muttered.

"Maybe you should rethink this," I said quietly.

Cameron's head swiveled in my direction. "Lia, we've gone over this. I have thought about it. Over and over again. I've dreamed about this possibility. Ever since I found out Calliope was a faery, I wondered what that would be like. Do you know how difficult it was to watch her leave me behind? She's the closest thing I have to family. And now? Now, I have you. I'd rather risk the change than go back to my mundane life with a father who hardly knows I exist, and two roommates who are only my friends because we have to live together. *This*," he cupped my face, "is the life I want."

I nodded and tried not to cry. How did we get here? How was it possible for my heart to feel so strongly so fast?

"All right."

"All right." His mouth turned up before he kissed me.

Kai returned with what I assumed was a stellvial. I'd never seen one used before, nor had I a reason to need one. It was almost identical to what the elves had used, except theirs had a metal needle on the end, whereas the stellvial was made purely of glass.

"Won't that break?" Cameron asked.

"Glass here isn't as fragile as it is in the human world," Calliope answered him and took the stellvial from Kai. "I worried about the same thing with my crown when I accidently dropped it while getting ready one morning. Not one crack."

"There is no risk of breaking it," Evan assured. "I promise it is as strong as metal."

"Let's get this over with. I can't wait any longer." Cameron stepped up to Calliope next to the table with the blood securely encased in a glass urn. "I'm ready."

"I don't know what I'm doing," Calliope panicked. "Evan, will you do it?"

"Your Highness, I have no more experience than you."

"But maybe your hands will shake less."

He lifted his frail hands as if that were an answer.

"Good grief, I'll do it." I stepped up and took the stellvial from Calliope. "Now, this isn't going to feel good," I said quietly to Cameron. "Your entire body is going to feel like it's on fire. It's going to feel like the new blood is burning away the old blood, which I guess it kind of is."

He nodded. "Cool. So, you have to stab me in the heart. There's possibility of death and horrible side effects, and it's going to burn like a mother until I transform." He took a deep breath, and then released it. "Got it. Let's do this."

"Maybe we should have him lay down." As soon as the blood kicked in he wasn't going to be able to stand.

"The window seat," Calliope suggested.

When Cameron was comfortably on his back, Calliope

helped me fill the stellvial with approximately the same amount of blood that had been used for me. I prayed to the fallen fae I was right.

"I'm going to apologize in advance. I'll do this quickly, but within seconds you'll be unconscious. Remember, the fire ends."

When he nodded and closed his eyes, I placed the needle over his heart and quickly pressed down. Cameron's face contorted in agony. I knew that pain all too well. His mouth opened, but there was no sound. It was the worst kind of pain. No sound could express the level of suffering.

Any moment his body would go limp.

Any second.

Just one more.

Cameron's eyes clamped shut. He hadn't taken a single breath. He wasn't going unconscious. *Why isn't it working?*

"Why hasn't he lost consciousness yet?" Calliope snapped.

"I don't know!"

I gently touched his face and brushed his hair from his forehead. "Cameron, it's almost over," I soothed, lying. I had no clue. "Just breathe. It'll all be over soon."

Was this what it'd looked like when the bodies couldn't withstand the change? Was I going to lose him? Tears pierced my eyes as he writhed back and forth. His voice began to work, and I wished it hadn't. His screams resonated throughout the atrium. Keepers on the other side of the castle could hear him.

I wanted it to stop. *I take it back.* Changing him wasn't worth the risk. I'd rather have an alive, human Cameron than one who no longer existed.

I was going to lose him. Would it be over soon?

"It'll all be over soon," I whispered.

And then it was.

THIRTY EIGHT

CAMERON

Death was an interesting experience. For some reason, I'd always thought I would go painlessly. I'd go at an old age, in my sleep, after living a long life.

I'd experienced the opposite of that. First, I'd felt an inferno light inside of me, and then I'd felt numb. There had been nothing but darkness. Every time I'd opened my eyes, there was nothing. I was nothing. I'd waited to wake up in front of the pearly gates, but it never happened. I hadn't been that bad of a human being, had I? Was I going to Hell? Was this Hell?

When the fire had receded from my veins, I'd laid there, numb for hours—it'd seemed—until it'd gradually withdrew as well. I'd remained still, savoring the pleasure of feeling alive and pain-free. Pain-free. If I were in Hell, surely there would be pain. Lots of fire and emptiness. All things horrible. Not this. I'd felt well-rested and strong.

I'd opened my eyes again and blinked at the bright light all around me. I *had* made it to heaven. Thank goodness. That would really have sucked.

When my vision cleared, and the light became less blinding, Lia loomed above me, smiling, with tears in her eyes.

Was this heaven?

"Cameron," she breathed and kissed me over and over. "Oh my gosh. You're awake."

What happened? Why was Lia kissing me?

"You were asleep for a day. I kept checking your pulse to make sure you were still alive. I was so scared."

"Scared of what?"

She looked at me funny. "That you wouldn't survive the change."

My heart began to race. What was she talking about? What had changed? Why wouldn't I have survived? Where am I? I lifted my head and looked around. Windows. Lots of windows. And sunlight and trees. Everything looked clear. So clear, like I was looking through the eyes of someone with the best vision on the planet.

"Cameron?" I knew that voice. Calliope appeared next to Lia.

"Oh, thank the Fallen Fae!" She grabbed me and hugged me tight. "Oh, sorry!" She quickly pulled back. "I shouldn't hug you so tight. Are you all right? Does anything hurt? Can I get you anything?"

"No, I'm fine." I sat up. Lia and Calliope looked at me like I was going to break.

"My hug didn't hurt you?" My mind was reeling. It didn't hurt. Normally, Calliope's hugs were so tight I couldn't breathe. Why didn't it hurt?

I shook my head. I needed quiet. There was too much to take in. Everything was too colorful, too sharp. Sensory overload. I closed my eyes. That was better.

"Cameron?" Lia asked, her voice shaky.

I held up a finger. I needed a minute. I could remember only bits and pieces. It was like my brain was shielding me, or I needed to shield it. Calliope and Lia wouldn't stop talking to each other. It sounded like a bunch of people were pacing outside the room. I could hear hundreds of people whispering and trees creaking and swaying and—

"AHH!" I placed my hands over my ears to block out the sounds, and jumped. My ears! I had points on my ears!

With wide eyes, I found Calliope. "I have points on my ears!"

"Cam, you're freaking out. This is a *good* thing. You survived the change. You didn't die! You're a faery!" She jumped up and down.

The change. The change. The change.

Holy crap! I'm a faery!

I grabbed my ears, tracing the tips. "They feel so real!"

She laughed. "Because they are, dork."

My eyes found Lia. She hovered off to the side, her hands rubbing anxiously together. In three steps I took her into my arms and pressed my mouth to hers. When I pulled back, she hit me in the chest.

I chuckled, "Ouch!"

"You scared me, you idiot! For a second, I thought you'd lost all your memories." Her chest heaved with her elevated breathing. "You looked at me like you didn't know who I was."

I traced the curve of her face. She was so beautiful. "I just needed a minute. I'm on a bit of sensory overload right now. I'm hoping I'll get used to it and it will wear off."

"It should," Calliope said. "For me, everything came in gradually, so I was able to absorb each change as it took place. Where you're experiencing it all at once. Who knows how much time it will take, but hopefully you'll be as be good as new soon."

"I hope so." I pressed my hand to the side of my head, massaging my temple. "I can hear everything."

They chuckled. Calliope started to back out of the atrium. "I'm going to leave you two. Kai will want to know the good news. Welcome to faerydom, Cam. Hopefully you love it, because you're kind of stuck here."

"I think I'll manage." I smiled as she walked out of the room.

I kept Lia in my arms, tightening around her waist. "So, what group do you think Sarai will put me in?"

"Group?"

"You know … the Keepers and Healers and stuff."

Lia laughed. Her head fell back. "You mean a colony."

"Yeah, that. What are you?"

"I'm a Sower."

"So, what do you do?"

"We handle the harvest. All the gardening and food, so our days are spent in the orchards and fields."

"So, a farmer." I nod. "I can do that. I can pull off the flannel and denim. That's a normal fad around here, right?" I smirked, and Lia bit back her smile. "Cameron the Farmer. Has a nice ring to it, don't you think?"

"You might want to keep the nicknames to yourself." She

kissed me lightly, and the corners of her eyes turned down, troubled. "In all seriousness, are you okay? Your transformation was horrifying. I know the pain you went through, but watching you suffering, I think it may have been worse for you than any other."

I'd never let Lia know the extent of the pain. She didn't need to know I'd thought I was dead, and in Hell, no less. I'd take that tidbit to my grave. She only needed to know one thing.

"I would do it a thousands times over if it meant I could have you."

THIRTY NINE

SARAI

The Keepers escorted me to the Oraelian court to meet the king and queen. Towering double doors were open when we approached. King Ronan and Queen Aislinn sat in adjoining thrones at the end of the great hall. Marcus stood beside Aislinn, while another stood next to Ronan. I could only assume he was Marcus's older brother, Alston, considering he looked identical to Marcus.

The Keepers led me all the way to the base of the thrones, and one announced my presence. "Sarai, Queen of Rymidon."

"King Ronan. Queen Aislinn." I bowed.

"Sarai." Marcus's voice was breathless.

"Marcus." I nodded to acknowledge him. His brother remained silent.

"For what do we owe the honor, Queen Sarai?" Queen Aislinn asked, her face serene and welcoming.

"I came to offer a trade agreement. But first, I was hoping to have a private moment with Prince Marcus. We have some unfinished business to attend to."

The King and Queen gave me questioning looks. Did they know where Marcus was when he was not present? Were they unaware Marcus and I had formed a connection? Did they know about the elves? Surely, not.

"Of course, my dear." Queen Aislinn regained herself first and smiled. She peered at Marcus. It was clear he was to answer to her when we were finished. *What will he say to her? How will he explain our situation?* He could worry about that. It wasn't my place.

Marcus was hesitantly optimistic when I caught his eye. "Let us go for a walk in the gardens," he suggested.

When we were outside the castle walls, he spoke up. "I didn't expect you to come. I was hoping to hear from you, but I feared it was unlikely."

"I wasn't planning to come, but I have a very persuasive sister."

"I am a lucky man for that." A smiled played on his lips.

"I think it is best to wait for phrases such as that until we are finished with this conversation."

The smile faded, and I felt a twinge of guilt for taking away his hope. For taking away one of his rare smiles. "Fair enough."

We walked in silence. The longer it lengthened, I knew I needed to say what I came to say, but I could not find the words. We reached a break in the pathway and Marcus gestured, asking with his hand, which way I wanted to go.

I did not move. I turned and looked up at him. "I forgive you, Marcus."

He heaved a sigh, a breath I knew he'd been holding since the moment I'd arrived unannounced. He stepped closer, but I put up my hand to ward him off.

"I forgive you, but I do not trust you."

His face fell, but he nodded. "I understand. It would surprise me if you did. I will prove myself to you. Whatever it takes."

Marcus came closer again, reaching out, and I stepped back. The hurt in his eyes caused me to turn away. It was too much to endure.

"While I do not agree with your actions, I have a better understanding of the path you chose. I will give you the chance to prove your trustworthiness, but I cannot be with you. I need time. Right now, my kingdom needs me. I cannot balance putting Rymidon back together while attempting to build a relationship with another Royal. Both would suffer, and neither could afford it."

"But a kingdom runs better with two. What will the counsel say about you holding off bonding? Or will you choose another?"

"I don't know, but I will fight to stand on my own for as long as they will allow. Rymidon has been through too much. With the elves relocating … Rymidon needs a focused queen and you distract me, Marcus."

It was difficult enough being in his presence. Looking at him made me want to change my mind. I would not be so weak.

"I want to accept your words, but they're painful. I understand why I stand where I do, but I don't want to accept it. Please, Sarai. I cannot bear to see you belong to anyone else."

Taken aback, I retorted, "I am no one's but my own."

He swooped in and gently clutched my shoulders. "You're right. Which is why the thought of you with another is so unbearable. You deserve someone who will be your equal, whose sole purpose is to bring you happiness. I wish I had made that my purpose when we first met. If I had, you would look at me with a smile instead of tears in your eyes." Marcus paused, his gaze searching mine. "I don't know where to go from here."

My voice shook when I said, "Your purpose will come."

He spun away. His hands gripped the back of his neck. "What have I done?" he whispered into the wind.

After being so angry with him, it was strange that all I wanted was to bring him comfort. "Marcus, if not for you, we would not have gotten to the elves in time. They could have an entire enhanced army raiding every kingdom."

"If not for me, the elves would've been discovered sooner, and you would still trust me."

I could not discount his rebuttal, but I didn't want to leave him on such hopeless terms.

"Give us time. I am not telling you no. I am telling you not now."

"But, you also are not telling me yes to a future."

"I am telling you maybe. It is all up to you. What kind of king do you want to be, Marcus? One who acts on vengeance and makes irrational decisions from passion-based emotions, the kind of king fae fear and cannot trust? Or do you want to be the kind of king who can stand strong and reasonable in the face of danger, the kind of king fae admire and look to for security? I want the kind of king by my side that I can trust and admire. Be him, and I will never leave your side."

Marcus breathed deep and fixated his green eyes on me. "I will strive to be him every day for you, Sarai."

"Then the possibility of our future is already brighter."

ACKNOWLEDGEMENTS

Just when I think I'm done with Faylinn, it pulls me back in.

Thank you, Regina Wamba, who created another gorgeous Faylinn cover!

Thank you, Madison Seidler, my editor, who's got my grammatical and punctuation back.

Michele, my books would take a lot longer to write without you and your daily encouragement and words.

Jessica, you magical unicorn, you. Thank you for always being there even when life gets crazy and in the way.

Thanks to my family goes without saying, but thank you nonetheless!

And Ryan, thanks for being so sexy, and wonderful, and always an inspiration. (You're welcome.)

To my readers, Faylinn keeps living on because of you. Thank you for loving these characters. I have so much love in my heart for you.

ALSO BY MINDY HAYES

The Faylinn Novels:
Kaleidoscope
Ember
Luminary

Willowhaven Series:
Me After You
Me Without You

YA Standalone
The Day That Saved Us

Co-written with Michele G. Miller
Paper Planes and Other Things We Lost

ABOUT THE AUTHOR

MINDY HAYES is the youngest of six children and grew up in San Diego, California. After graduating from Brigham Young University-Idaho, she discovered her passion for reading and writing.. Mindy and her husband have been married for nine years and live in Summerville, South Carolina.

You can visit Mindy online:
www.mindyhayes.com
www.facebook.com/hayes.mindy

19987464R00130

Printed in Great Britain
by Amazon